The Sunshine
When She's Gone

The Sunshine When She's Gone

A NOVEL

THEA GOODMAN

HENRY HOLT AND COMPANY NEW YORK

Henry Holt and Company, LLC
Publishers since 1866
175 Fifth Avenue
New York, New York 10010
www.henryholt.com

Henry Holt® and ® are registered trademarks of
Henry Holt and Company, LLC.

Copyright © 2013 by Thea Goodman
All rights reserved.

The song "Kingston Town" by Kendrick Patrick; Copyright © Sparta Florida Music
Group, Ltd. (BMI) International Copyright Secured. All Rights Reserved.
Reprinted by Permission of Embassy Music Corporation (BMI).

Library of Congress Cataloging-in-Publication Data
Goodman, Thea.
The sunshine when she's gone: a novel / Thea Goodman.—1st ed.
    p.   cm.
ISBN 978-0-8050-9662-0
 1. Parenting—Psychological aspects—Fiction.   2. Marriage—Psychological
aspects—Fiction.   I. Title.
PS3607.O59223S86 2013
813'.6—dc23

                                                                              2012027373

Henry Holt books are available for special promotions and
premiums. For details contact: Director, Special Markets.

First Edition 2013

Designed by Kelly S. Too

Printed in the United States of America
1   3   5   7   9   10   8   6   4   2

This is a work of fiction. All of the characters, organizations, and events portrayed
in this novel either are products of the author's imagination or are used fictitiously.

For Eric

The Sunshine
When She's Gone

PART ONE

FLIGHT

1

Thursday Night

John

Kidnap was not the right word. John had simply meant to take Clara to breakfast at the corner diner, where they had good poached eggs and were especially kind to babies. But in the end he couldn't explain the inexorable pull, the electric thrum that made him rise from the bed, strangely untethered, and begin to shave with scalding water, or the innocence of his motive—*he just wanted to be with her.* He couldn't describe the indefinite urgency that had propelled him. Yes, he took the baby with him, but she was his daughter.

Veronica had started it. She'd sat up in bed, waving a finger in protest. "She's fine," she'd hissed when John left to check on Clara, as he did every night. Clara slept down the hall, in a nursery with walls the color of pollen. They'd rejected *bicycle yellow* and *lemon yellow* in favor of *pollen*, the potent reproductive center of a flower. As he walked toward the nursery, a small vibration filled the air, the joyful tension that had tinged the atmosphere since Clara was born. The yolky color summoned, spilling warmth onto the stunned concrete floors and his cold bare feet: The baby was warm and breathing. He was sure of it. When he arrived in her room, it was pitch dark. He felt around the baseboards, searching in vain for the delinquent night-light, then stood staring down at the vague shape of the crib but saw only blackness, like the deep velvet center of a pansy. Had she been stolen?

He waited anxiously for his eyes to adjust to the dark. Slowly the shape of her bald head emerged, and he saw a fantastic, tuber-like arm draped over her eyes as she lay on her back. He watched, waiting to see her chest move up and down with breath. Abruptly, she flipped over. In her pink velour suit, her bottom was high in the air, her tiny knees tucked beneath her. In the crook of her arm she had crushed the lamb she loved. The velvety white toy had opaque black eyes and eyebrows embroidered in perpetual consternation, as if forever on the verge of bleating. But the baby was content tonight. Neither Clara nor the lamb made a sound.

Satisfied, he returned to their pale blue bedroom. What was the name of this paint color? They had once been fervent and focused decorators. He had once agreed to the color, but it was a drained blue, gray and institutional, the bored whistle in the stairwell of his old elementary school. Veronica was speaking, staring across the top of her book into the open distance, barely aware of his presence. "There's an epidemic under way. People are getting fatter and fatter," she said.

John's waist had thickened for the first time in his life, and he supposed this was why she avoided contact. "Obesity is a scourge," he said too emphatically. His provocation didn't faze her. Veronica arranged her maple hair over the pillow—the same glossy banner she'd always had, so shiny it looked adolescent—and continued to read about the horror of fast food. She held a tissue coned into one nostril and worked on arranging it for optimal absorption. He'd never seen her so engaged.

She was in shape again, six months after Clara's birth, but complained of the continual numbness of her incision and the lack of tone around her belly. He'd find her alone sometimes, her side to the mirror, lifting the small packet of flesh above the ridge of the scar until taut, then dropping it as it jiggled back into place and froze into a small, immovable pillow. She'd be embarrassed when he found her doing this and rush to cover herself. He liked seeing her in that moment when she didn't know she was being seen. She'd never been vain *before*. Maybe it wasn't vanity; she still had little sense of the power of her beauty, an innocence that had always been one of her charms.

"Hi," he said, trying to take her book away and kiss her. Art, his closest friend, had always said *hi* was a good opener. No one could say no to *hi*.

"Don't," she said. She looked at his hand briefly, as if disoriented, her watery violet eyes narrowing. "What are you doing?"

"Kissing you." He leaned in, waiting for her to remove the tissue.

She stared at the page before her. "The thing is"—she coughed vigorously, then recovered—"I'm really sick." A plane of red chafed skin seared above her chapped lips, but he didn't care.

"Where's your puritan stoicism these days?" John grabbed the tissue box and stuffed his hand inside it. He lifted up his cubed fist as if admiring it. *Before*, Veronica was someone who ignored colds, too busy to slow down and nurse one.

Clara had divided all experience into *before* and *after*. Before, his wife was stalwart, even hearty; after, she was withholding and often sick. On occasion, she had been perhaps oversensitive; now she was brittle. Before, she had been pleasure-loving and absentminded, one time stowing her purse in the refrigerator—as if enthralled by the present, the current consuming thing, which had often been him! After, she continued to work at the Commission for School Lunches, and she talked about murals and community gardens and smoking bans yet spoke with a new, almost officious fervor. After, her work and her interests surrounded her like a fence. He couldn't get in.

"Give me that," she said, reaching for the box as he moved his hand away.

"You need to do something about it," he said.

"About my cold? I'm trying to blow my nose," she said, with her new, caustic bite.

"It's not your nose I'm worried about," he said, pausing to admire the almost aquiline line of it, the terse, receptive pink tip jammed with tissues. Veronica almost smiled, until something made him keep going and ruin it. "It's your mood. You're so moody."

She snatched the box off his hand, revealing his red clenched fist. "Don't tell me what I am. You don't know!" she said. "You have no idea, none at all, how tired I am."

"Of course I know." He spoke quietly, a patient robot, tired to the point of malfunction.

Sleep—for both of them—had become a precious commodity, worthy of fetish. They discussed sleep. They were always counting the consecutive hours of sleep they'd had or calculating the few they could hope for. He, too, was wrecked. As she glared at him, the accumulated exhaustion of months seemed to calcify within him, then crack. He was buzzing; he was blanched. How could she suppose he didn't know fatigue?

At six months, Clara had not once slept through the night. He told himself this circumstance was temporary—if Veronica would let Clara into their room, out of the inky dark of the nursery (draped in three-ply blackout shades), then the baby might sleep. For now he dwelled in a bright flip book of days and a tunnel of nights that kept returning like an endless boomerang to pull him in, thread him through to the next impossible morning. They'd entered into a syndrome of tiredness that seemed as if it would never end. "I do know," he repeated in as measured and human a tone as he could muster.

Her eyes grew large with pity, like a school psychologist with a hopeless case.

"Don't look at me like that," he said, "that condescending smile."

"I'm not even looking at you." It was true. She was already back to her book and spoke in her new monotone. They were both robots. A pair of imposters. "Why don't you take care of your mood and I'll take care of mine?"

"My mood?" he said. "I can't even say anything—I can't even come near you—"

"So that's what this is about. I'm at least trying to do something about it," she said, gesturing to the prescription bottles on the bedside table—the cluster of antidepressants and the hormones for her waning sex drive. "I know you'd like to think it's entirely chemical, but there's more to it than that," she added. "Show me one new mother who actually wants to have sex."

"Last time you were just servicing me? Is that it?" Over and over he had recalled that last uncommon encounter, three weeks ago, when he'd managed to capture her as she stacked some clean towels in the linen closet.

"I wanted to." She reached out and squeezed his biceps. The gesture softened him. His muscle twitched happily beneath her long fingers. "I just don't want to all the time. Why are you yelling at me?" Her hand rose, left him.

"I'm not. I'm sorry."

"You think it's all me, but it's you too," she said, as if in a trance. She turned a page and stifled a sneeze. He looked up. Even the ceiling was blue—what had the idea been? The painted ceiling was meant to feel limitless, like the sky, but it was laughably hard and unyielding.

"Me? You're blaming me?" he said, sure that her hormones were dividing them, turning her into a person she had not been before, someone alternately aloof, despondent, and cutting. He waited, stewing. Indignation prickled up through his scalp. It felt purifying, a bubbly thing, like peroxide poured onto a wound. She had changed since the birth; he had not.

That enormous night when *before* turned into *after*, a nurse had addressed John and said, "Say goodbye, Dad," escorting him out of the operating room where Veronica had given birth by C-section. He'd pressed his lips to Veronica's damp forehead. Despite her waxy pallor, she'd smiled at him bravely, as if nothing and no one would ever hurt or disappoint her; to that hopeful essence of his wife—whether real or imaginary— he said goodbye. The heavy door clicked behind him.

A baby, placid and trusting, had been placed in his arms. She felt too light at first, a hollow doll wrapped in flannel, but when he adjusted his wrist, her warm head fell back heavily. He gathered her together, her delicate, watery, animated weight. He couldn't tell if she looked like Veronica. He searched the baby's face for traces of his own, but there were none. Her face was a mobile rosebud, like any baby's. "There's a theory," he told the nurse who was restocking the cabinet beside him, "that newborns look like their fathers so their fathers won't eat them."

"The cafeteria is on three. I can take baby to the nursery while you eat," she said, continuing her work. He watched her uniformed back as she reached a high shelf on tiptoe. *Take baby?* If Veronica was going to be all right, she would have looked him in the eye.

"No," he said, unaccountably angry. "It's a *theory* . . . of evolutionary biology." He stared down at Clara as if she might get it. She opened her eyes briefly, then raised one eyebrow in exactly the way he did. With Clara's raised brow, time raced forward and fell back in an instant, a vacuumed second in which he understood the *Universe*. He understood, in a thread-bare yet distinct way, like a sighted person reading lips, that she was his daughter. A second later he saw no resemblance. The moment of recognition was not that clear: What he saw was not a small John but a resonance. He looked into Clara's no-color eyes and she melted warmly into his arms. He smiled at her within their unified haze, amid a deep yet sure abstraction that he recognized, quite suddenly, was love.

In the bedroom six months later, Veronica turned her back to him and flicked off her lamp. He lay beside her, listening while her jagged breath deepened into sleep. He couldn't rest. Light from unknown city sources shimmied on the walls. Exhaustion coated him, threatening to pull him under its sway several times, until a shimmering commenced, like pepper in his brain, shaking him awake. He stared at Veronica's shoulder, so smooth it looked oiled, at her elegant long fingers and that girlish hair, wishing she'd wake up and return to him. The hours of sleep he'd anticipated diminished one by one as he listened for the baby's cry; for once she was content.

When the sanitation trucks groaned over the cobblestone, he knew it was too late to sleep. Naked, he perched on the windowsill. The sun had not risen, but the sky was getting lighter. The apartment was silent. Clara had done it, had slept through the night. It was the end of an era. Chilly air outlined his body, sharpening his contours. Accidentally, his hand brushed a cactus.

He pricked his finger and squeezed it, waiting to see a drop of blood. Sucking the wound, he stared out the bedroom window. Lavender snow dusted the jumbled rooftops of Lafayette Street and in the distance, uptown, the gem-like facets of the Chrysler Building gleamed. New York was still impossibly beautiful. He wandered to the kitchen searching for some unknown object he'd misplaced, then without finding or even remembering it, moved to the living room's western exposure. It was a true loft, without corner windows, and he faced the one-time factory across the street, where a dark shape, perhaps a cat, rested against a pane. Opening the window, he leaned out and looked south until he could see the blank space where the towers, almost four years later, were still gone.

It had turned into another futuristic year: 2005. An apocalyptic wind surrounded him. The cold and adrenaline made his chest a net of lit veins. The city was vigorously rebounding and he was part of it. At thirty-five, John could do as he pleased. A former journalist, he was now a well-paid researcher for a successful hedge fund. He was their anonymous know-it-all, gathering information about companies and CEOs and delivering it to the principals. He was a good student, writing research papers for jocks. At best he felt like a private detective. Yes, he had achieved a certain ease, more than he'd ever known as a writer, but almost missed—what was it? The ego, the meager reward of a byline? These days he had money and, by extension, unprecedented freedom. Pinballs zoomed and bounced within him. He was rich. The baby slept through the night. There was no such thing as fatigue. The world was starting anew. His muscles were wound tight as a spring, ready for release. In this glorious state, his body was persuasive; he was not falling asleep, he was waking up, he was soaring. Up, up, and away he'd fly.

He went to the bathroom—as tightly decked with veined gray marble as a small Italian bank—and turned on the faucet, letting the water steam in the basin. Although he hadn't slept, he moved with slow precision. Each stroke of the razor scraped away a layer of skin cells until he was peeled and pristine, a shaved man in a cartoon dream. He was sure of one thing: He would not go in to Miller Equities today. He arrived there every day and did his research in situ, providing the information when the principals needed it—*scenarios,* they called them—reported from the virtual ether of the Web. Yes, Lloyd Miller routinely nodded at him at the morning meeting or in the hall, but John's physical presence seemed irrelevant, and he'd often wondered why he couldn't work at home. The idea took hold and bloomed; he would play hooky. He thought of coffee steaming in a thick china mug. First he'd take Clara for a walk to celebrate her success. Quickly, he got dressed.

It was still dark in the nursery. The air purifier stood sentinel in its corner, emitting small clouds of steam. He picked up Clara's floppy lamb—in sleep she had released it—and tucked its legs into his pants pocket. He put on the baby carrier, making sure the X was in the center of his back for proper weight distribution, then scooped up the baby and slipped her warm body into the pouch on his chest, where she remained asleep. He was embarrassed by the novelty of her weight, how solid and round she now felt. He wondered how long it had been since he'd carried her this way, as he put on his down jacket and zipped it around them both so he was huge.

He filled a backpack with a few bottles of the special homemade goat-milk formula Veronica had learned to make from an expensive herbalist on lower Fifth Avenue. He took diapers and wipes and a few extra onesies. In the hallway he put a hat on Clara and took some cash from a drawer in the console; Veronica said it reminded her of *The Godfather,* keeping cash in a drawer. But he liked the drawer and took much more than he needed, a little stack of crisp twenties and even a few fifties.

He grabbed a long-neglected pile of mail and put it in the bag to peruse at breakfast. Then he dashed off a note—a small good thing they still did for each other—leaving it on the kitchen island.

Outside, the January air was bracing; ice and salt cracked beneath his boots. A distance away he heard the click of a woman's heels but when he turned saw no one. He would get the poached eggs, and Clara would play with the toast points. They'd sit in the red leather booth. He jiggled her up the block, racing to get out of the cold. When he got to the corner, he cupped his hands to peer through the dark glass of the restaurant. The diner was closed. A wind of desolation whipped at his neck. All around him, old garbage and dirty snow banked the sidewalks like small mountain ranges that would never melt. He turned south toward the hole in the skyline, past the stores. There were so few galleries in Soho now; they'd been replaced by fancy shops. Veronica, with her master's in modern art, said she minded this, but she didn't. Who was he to talk? He stacked cash in a drawer *just in case.* They lived a material life, yet an edge of possibility breathed within it: His reflection in a store window showed the impossible silhouette of a pregnant man. He laughed, his breath steaming in staccato clouds in front of him, then hurried toward Broome Street, looking for someplace that was open.

By the time he reached Canal, the cold was inescapable. Clara burrowed into his chest and he wrapped his arms around her, both daunted and emboldened by her helplessness. The wet wind and intermittent hail bit at his face. An empty cab ambled by. He flagged it down and jumped in. The car was perfectly warm, nicely sealed, and smelled of mint. Sitar music began as a thin sheet of freezing rain glazed the windows. "Where are you headed?" a voice asked.

"Uptown."

But uptown, Arthur would be asleep, and Ines would be angry if John showed up before breakfast. The Museum of Natural History was closed, the butterflies still. He kissed the baby's fat, chilly hand, trying to remember the last time he'd been alone with her. He steamed her cold ear with his breath to warm her up, craving an inversion, the opposite of winter. "Actually, go west here," he said near Carmine Street, thinking of a diner he and Veronica used to go to after late nights in the Meatpacking District. "Little West Twelfth Street."

As the cab driver wound his way through the tangle of the West Village, John sorted the mail. He found a thick envelope from the passport agency; he'd commandeered the whole family to the downtown office one morning for passports and then dim sum, arguing that they'd go away eventually. He looked for his renewal first. His eyes were clear amber, deadpan, almost criminally expressionless. Veronica looked suspiciously happy in hers, her smile too white above the blue scarf at her throat. In Clara's photo he admired the single pale tuft of sparse hair (it had since fallen out), the peachy globe of her cheek, her bright dark-blue eyes vaguely crossed as she lay on a white sheet; the same photo she would use for five years.

The driver turned down the music to concentrate, crept around Jane Street, and funneled onto Eighth Avenue. Large flakes of snow began to cluster in the sky and swirl around the car as it moved cautiously. The car grew chilly. John fiddled with the air vent, trying to get more heat. As he leaned forward to tell the driver how to get to the restaurant, he saw that the windshield had whitened completely. The wipers squeaked into motion.

Somewhere in the world the sky was blue, the air was warm. Far away, the sun poured down like gold, melting knots in shoulders, warming hair, making things grow.

"If you could go back," he said, "to Crosby Street—" The car inched through the gray, clotted streets then sped down Varick. But as they drove east on Canal, past the first fleet of commuters emerging from the Holland Tunnel, the early trucks with Chinese letters creaking under their own weight, as they rolled quietly over the cushion of snow, he marveled at the speed of transportation, the remarkable will of all these travelers: To deliver star fruit to Canal Street, to deliver bread to Mott, to leave a quiet New Jersey lawn and jump into the fray, and at the end of the day to jump *out* of the fray. To jump out of the fray. This frozen season could vanish, revealing the brightness of the next. He was not ready to go home, and the driver, as if in accord, was lost. They slipped onto Bowery and then to the faded grandeur of Delancey. Up ahead there was the Williamsburg Bridge, a magical leap over the water, and before John had told himself what he was doing, he told the driver the way he liked to get to Kennedy.

"Foreign or domestic?" The driver's eyes waited like two dark gems in the rearview mirror. To the right of the mirror, he'd taped a photo of a child in pink footie pajamas. There were certain universal joys. For a beat the street beneath them was seamless, an inimical gray dream, dotted as far as John could see with green lights.

"Foreign."

2

Friday Morning

Veronica

Veronica stretched her arms with relief. She swept her legs, straight as the shadow on a sundial, across the empty bed. John had left and Clara was still asleep. Eyes closed, she felt the incision with her fingers. The scar was insensate, as if it belonged to someone else. She needed to get up and check on Clara, to change her diaper and make her bottle, but the pillow and the pale blue sheets were so comfortable, and having the bed to herself was rare. Even as Veronica lay there, luxuriating in a few minutes of rest, she longed to see Clara. She strained to hear her new early-morning babble, but the air was still, silent.

The quiet felt full, a rest in music, and she turned to the clock. *Eight?* The baby must have slept through the night. But *eight?* Eight was hilarious. Impossible. The clock must have stopped the night before, while she was pretending to read about obesity. Clara always cried before six. John always left for work before the baby woke up for the day. The mornings, *all* the early mornings, were hers. She rushed into the nursery, squinting amid the sunny yellow walls. The white crib, a Swedish thing, bare and unadorned, sat lower to the ground than most, over the sheepskin rug, in case, Veronica had reasoned, Clara fell out. She peered inside it. The baby was gone. Even the beloved lamb was gone. Fully awake, Veronica darted out of the room and into the kitchen, the buffed concrete floor chilly on her feet. She found a mint-green sticky note on the marble counter:

> *Dear V,*
> *I know you said you could use a break.*
> *Feel better.*
> *It's good to watch you finally sleep.*
> *Love, John (and C)*

He'd signed his name with a flourish, a huge looping *J*, like a fifth-grader with dreams of fame. She smiled. It was gallant, unusually generous, but he had scared the hell out of her. Had she said she needed a break? She did need one, but it felt like stating the obvious to say this directly. *Watch you sleep* sounded vaguely romantic. She had slept well; the night had been dreamless and sound, a pure, unconscious spell that was long enough to restore a baseline, an absence of symptoms; joints that did not ache, eyes that were not sore, a mind that was opening like a dry sponge dropped in water. She picked up the sticky note. Her sinuses had cleared. She could appreciate romance now, having slept long and well.

But where was he? She filled the electric kettle and flicked it on. Before Clara, she'd adored John's spontaneity, but after the birth, his frenetic energy level, his impulsivity, seemed incommensurate with the demands of a new baby. They'd discovered the idea of *before* and *after* together, when they were still in the hospital, but now the notion only divided them.

After, he refused to see that Clara had subsumed their lives; after, he suggested ridiculous outings, that they dance capoeira—they never had before—or buy a tent and go camping. He didn't seem to realize that they weren't going anywhere.

Before, John had incorporated the prevailing, confused ethos for men of his generation—he was supposed to sometimes make dinner, he was to care about a choice of appliances, he was to transfer clothes from washer to dryer without having to be asked and even, sometimes, to vacuum—all the while focusing on the larger destiny, his career. After, it was as if—with the exception of his obsessive nightly visits to check on the baby—he'd forgotten what generation he was born in. He'd become consumed by his own appetites; he touched her not with sensitivity but with the impatient ardor of a teenage boy.

This morning he was giving her a break. She looked out the open kitchen, past the two pretentious Roman pillars, into the stark living room, as she poured coffee beans into the grinder. She could see that the red stroller was parked near the elevator, but the backpack, marketed as a special *men's* diaper bag, was gone. Being alone was an unsettling gift. She enjoyed the sudden release of tension in her neck and shoulders, the new lightness in her arms, even as she missed the warm weight and the improbably soft skin of her daughter. A bunch of spotted bananas rested on the counter. Two days ago Clara had celebrated her six-month birthday by tasting one.

Within the whirring sound of the coffee grinder, she shuddered; six months ago Veronica had been taken apart and put back together again. Her reproductive life had begun and ended in the same night. How could that have happened? Despite her great good fortune—she'd had a healthy baby; she had survived—she was left alone circling the question. The proof of her fertility existed, a separate being with growing energy. She had made a person. All day long, even at work, she was dogged by Clara's existence; the baby amazed her, with her transparent fingernails as tiny and round as lentils, the swell of her torso that contained a perfect set of organs, the way she had just begun, when excited, to twirl her fat wrists like a flamenco dancer.

Veronica couldn't stop herself from calling John. When she got his voice mail, she spoke quickly. "Hi. I guess you're going in late. Thanks for letting me sleep in. Give me a call and let me know where you guys are, okay?" The kettle whistled briefly before she turned it off and poured it onto the dark grounds. Through the water's steam she looked out the window; the sky was a troubled charcoal gray. Fine needles of hail rattled the panes. Disintegrate. How did one *integrate*? She played the words over and over in her mind. There was the night, the literal bodily rupture, and the rupture in time; everything since—the feel of water on her hands at the sink, the sweet, nutty breath of her daughter, food that had become mere sustenance—came to her in broken pieces. Twenty minutes here. Four minutes there. Experience was chopped and disconnected. She shook her head to dispel the tumble of thoughts, the vast effort of connecting it all. Suddenly she was very tired again. She peered into the bedroom: The soothing blue walls beckoned; the sheets had a satiny sheen. She would just go rest for another minute, as the coffee steeped, no more.

She lay down, wrapping her arms around her shoulders like a girl pretending to be kissed. How long had it been since she'd been kissed that deeply, in the way that children parody? Chilly, she put a pillow over her shoulders: A blanket would be an acknowledged commitment to nap. Still, she fell.

Veronica was floating and contained, a flute in a velvet case: lithe and strong and capable of beauty. Slowly, the velvet fell away. Noise perforated a vanishing dream. A distant car alarm sounded. Somewhere a clothes dryer shook endlessly. She opened her eyes and for a moment had no idea where she was.

The dry cactus dying on a windowsill, the smear of shark-oil eye cream on the pillowcase: She recognized those first. (She and Ines had succumbed to the whole skin-care line one Saturday morning at Barneys.) She checked the time. A decadent nine-fifteen! She laughed at her unlikely delinquency. Ordinarily by this time she'd have combed through the market's produce section, selected something green for dinner, found the herbs for Clara's formula, and sussed out possible organic vendors for the revamp of Jasper School lunches. Busy-ness. Yes, business was the antidote to her loop of obsessive discourse, to the thoughts about the parts. Clara was her reward, a perfect, healthy girl.

Nine-fifteen. The prospect of their nanny, Rosemary's, mild scolding got her out of bed. Veronica showered carefully, for once not rushing, taking time to condition her hair, then moisturize her ashy knees and floss her teeth. By the time she remade the coffee, which had become cold, and finished her oatmeal, Rosemary still hadn't appeared. Clara's nap was in fifteen minutes. Veronica dialed Rosemary's cell, her heart galloping.

"Hi. Good morning, Rosemary."

"Hello, missus!"

"I'm just wondering if you met up with them or—"

"It seems your husband is taking the day off with the baby, and he told me to head home," Rosemary said.

Veronica let her bowl clatter to the sink. "You didn't go, did you?" A shadow of pain flickered across her abdomen, like a running insect.

"I'm afraid I did."

"Well, where are they? Did he say where they were going?" She worried a damp finger over a spot of red wine that had stained the counter.

"I assume they're back home," Rosemary said, "for the nap." Veronica gave up on the stain and bit a cuticle. She twirled her engagement ring around her finger. A pretty diamond with twin baguettes. Sometimes when she glanced at it, all that platinum looked like a cavity flashing inside a molar. "Missus?"

"No, *I'm* here at home and they're not."

"He's gone off taking your baby, eh? American fathers are wonderful. They try to help, but they don't understand the importance of naptime. The *value* of the nap. There's a window of time to get her down and that's it. Men don't understand timing, is all, the importance of timing."

"So true." Veronica laughed, comforted by Rosemary's plati-
tude. Irish Catholic, fiftyish Rosemary, who could soothe Clara
instantly with her soft, powdery hands. Utterly capable Rosemary, with her attitude of deference and also mild superiority.

"I suppose I'll see you Monday, then?" Rosemary said.

"See you then."

As she hung up, Veronica was surprised by a longing for
Rosemary. As a child in the seventies, she'd spent long after-
noons watching her nanny, Kay, polish silver teapots or con-
vincing Kay to play one more game of Parcheesi. Did Kay
love her? She ordered Veronica's day. She fed her and bathed
her, providing all the crucial acts of daily sustenance.

Rosemary, too, had been constant witness and succor for
the past few months. Rosemary had even helped her shower
during those early weeks after the birth, as Veronica, on
heavy pain meds, stood unsteadily in her shattered body. When
Veronica had tried to nurse, despite an acute double mastitis,
and failed, Rosemary had been there, a bridge to the tiny,
curled infant girl with her raw stub of umbilical cord and her
ceaseless hunger.

When would John and Clara appear? She sprayed the coun-
ters and began to load the dishwasher, packing it with a new
fastidiousness. You could be disintegrated, you could suddenly feel like you were a hundred years old, but there were
these small consolations.

An easy birth, from the reports of her friends, was an oxy-
moron. And although a cesarean hysterectomy was fairly rare,
she knew stories far worse than her own. The problem wasn't
what had happened, wasn't merely the clinical facts of the
night; it was their mysterious and private—for no one else

thought about them—reverberation. The blue sheet had been in front of her face, too close, and the radio (*the radio!*) had been playing "Stairway to Heaven." As John left the operating room, her eyes fell to his blue shoe covers, the cloth over the toes darkened with blood.

After Clara, no wisdom bloomed with motherhood, despite her mother-in law's prediction. After, she was dumber, puffier, her concentration more transient. Where there had been intelligence now resided a massive cloud, a precipitous fuzzy thing that wouldn't just go ahead and fucking rain.

The kitchen was clean. The wind had died down. A fragile sun ascended, glowing across the floor, over the small colorful Tibetan rug, to the kitchen counter. Sunlight illuminated and barely warmed her hands as she leaned there, the days beginning to lengthen, the darkest part of winter gone. She had slept in and the world was altered.

She went into the bedroom and fastened the top button of her dress, an embroidered black kimono, then put a black leather belt over it. She applied mascara and picked up the hair dryer, but it felt too heavy, like a weapon in her hand. Before, she would have been quite interested in what the children at the Jasper School had for lunch. In a few months, she'd banished their vending machines. She'd siphoned iceberg lettuce off the menu and introduced the nutritious sprigs of watercress. Before, she had cared. She had cared about many things—Expressionist paintings and community gardens and slow food. What had been the meaning of her previous adult life, her two master's degrees (the second in public health), when nothing but the baby now truly captured her attention? Who was she if she was not interested? She was just this mammal, this warm mama.

"A *mammal?*" John had said, when Clara was a newborn. "You're a Botticelli." Her hair was center-parted, light brown with natural waves at the ends, like the nymphs'. But she hardly looked like a Botticelli. She was much tawnier, her skin less pink and more apricot. Lately she liked to recall the compliment, the feeling of being adored. Did he still notice her hair?

Out of habit, she pressed a button on her phone to call Ines, who was always reachable on her cell lately, always staring at her phone, waiting for the fertility clinic to call and tell her when to sleep with Art. Veronica couldn't ramble about disintegration to poor Ines, who remained trapped in a painful epic baby quest.

"Good news!" Ines said as she answered. "I'm eleven weeks!"

"Really?" Veronica sat down on the edge of her bed to absorb the news and bounced a little. Ines must have known for a long time without saying a word. They'd told each other everything since they'd met as Barnard freshmen more than fifteen years earlier. "When did you find out? Is Arthur excited?" Ines would now know this uncontainable, blowsy love.

"He's ecstatic."

"Amazing! My God, our kids will grow up together!" Clara might feel as if she had a sibling.

"Anyway, how are *you?*" Ines asked. Veronica hesitated. Maybe, just this morning, with Ines's good news and the extra sleep, she was *integrating;* Ines's lie was one of omission only. It would be childish to complain.

"Strange but good, I think. John let me sleep in this morning. That hasn't happened in so long and, for once, he didn't wake up Clara last night."

"That would drive me nuts. Can't you stop him?"

"I can't! He goes in sometimes when I'm already asleep." How Veronica wished she possessed Ines's force of personality. Ines would never let Arthur get away with this. "Listen, this is the best news, but I should probably get going. Clara's not back for her nap, and I need to find out where they are."

"No you don't. They're fine." Ines could be clipped and sharp, but Veronica appreciated this; Ines brought her onto a single plane devoid of ambivalence.

"You're right," she said, wanting to see Ines, to feel that solidity. "Do you want to meet tonight, to celebrate? I'm going to ask John to stay in with Clara." She was so refreshed by the extra sleep, by the unexpected gift of that nap.

"I'll cook you dinner," Ines said.

"Or we could go out." Veronica didn't want dinner at Ines's apartment; every time away from Clara was burdened with having to be a peak experience. But Ines remained free within her own home. And she had that blue ashtray and those neat joints she rolled expertly. Veronica wondered if she could smoke one, even though Ines couldn't. Ines told her to come over at seven. "I can't wait to see you . . . and congratulations."

When she left the building, the thin air sparkled with cold, wending its way into the hollows behind her knees, her scalp, and even her teeth. Her breath steamed. She paused when she saw a man pushing a stroller up the block. She wanted desperately for it to be Clara and John, and she fervently hoped it wouldn't be. If she saw Clara now, she would have to pick her up and hug her. She would press her face onto those sublime smooth cheeks, inhale, and not want to let her go. But no; the man that passed was Asian, the stroller was black. She turned at the end of the block, a little worried, but with each step she was freer and freer.

Soon she sat alone in the backseat of a cab speeding up Sixth Avenue. The driver wore a maroon turban and turned off the radio when she spoke. The prospect of the peaceful ten-minute ride with the sooty breeze blowing in her face soothed her. She lounged in the backseat. An ambulance startled her briefly with its foreboding blare. But when she looked out the window, the magic of sleep had applied a glimmer to the dirty snow, a sheen to the formerly gray sky, as if a window were opening within high walls.

3

Friday

John

The air was soft and warm and smelled of coconuts. John could feel it rolling down the aisle of the airplane when the doors were finally opened. Women exchanged their shoes for sandals. People peeled off their sweaters and put on their sunglasses. The winter dryness in his nasal passages, in his bones, melted away. Was it possible? John couldn't quite believe it. Holding the sleeping, sticky baby to his chest, he stepped out the door and stood for a moment at the top of the landing. The largest sky hung above him, heavy with puffy white clouds. He could see the airport and beyond that a group of cows munching on grass beneath trees permanently bent by the trade winds. Around the edges of the airport there was cotton, white down growing out of scrappy brown thorns. He walked down the stairs and across the glare of the tarmac. Inside the open building, humid breezes caressed his face and

arms. The customs officers were languid. Relaxation, or perhaps malaise, permeated the atmosphere. How could anyone
work here, where it smelled like sugar, where standing in the
breeze was so sensational that it felt like actually *doing* something?

The pretty caramel-skinned woman behind the counter
looked at the two passports then pursed her lips as she examined John's face. "Just the two of you? Without her mum?"

As John hesitated, the woman smirked. Or was she simply
smiling? He recalled a Caribbean way of teasing, of being
willfully indirect. "Without her mother, yes," was all he could
manage. The woman smiled. He'd been paranoid; she meant
no harm. They had no baggage and moved quickly out to a
line of taxis. The white tourists around him were donning
wide-brimmed hats and visors and applying zinc to their
noses. He liked to think that he and Clara were different, that
they weren't tourists but emissaries. He moved with the spirit
of a mission; for what cause, he couldn't say. His mood, the
high from the morning, felt a lot like being in love: irrational
and full of conviction. John felt he had to be here, that it was
inevitable, and there was nowhere else he and Clara could
have possibly gone.

His driver spoke about the weather. "It's been sunny, hot,
for some time, and the rainy season is probably over."

"What about those big clouds over there?"

"It rains a little bit every day—a shower," he was told. "No
big storm."

John was happy, exuberant. His heart pounded as if he'd
done a line of coke. He had a few times, years ago, with Arthur,
after pickup basketball games. Veronica claimed, then, to

have never liked drugs. He'd felt so good on those nights, powerful and unconfined. That omnipotence was back; here he was, in the Caribbean, in the coldest stretch of a New York winter.

Awake, Clara shimmered against him. He hadn't spent much time with her lately and was surprised by her constant movement, the tight compression of energy buzzing within her, the dynamic play of muscles in her face. "See the cows?" he asked her, pointing out the window. She grinned widely and kicked in response.

As tired as he was, he kept looking at her. As a child up way past his bedtime, he'd watched fireworks over the Hudson; his lids drooped with fatigue and then snapped open, in thrall to each colorful explosion. Clara's kicks and coos were as compelling as those streams of fire exploding in the sky.

They drove through miles of sugar cane. The pale-green stalks rose high above the chilly, air-conditioned white minivan. Veronica would have been appalled because there was no car seat. Instead, he'd pulled the seat belt over both of them as Clara bounced on his knees. The cane smelled sweet. Its walls created a green tunnel, with the back of the driver's shaved chocolate-colored head in the foreground and the twisting road ahead. When the cane petered out, the road went uphill, grew craggy and littered with stones. Goats wandered by, crying, *mama, mama.* Clara twirled her wrists in delight.

Her good nature had saved them. On the plane she had thrown up and then giggled. She had soaked through one diaper after another. When he'd carried her to the tiny bathroom to change her, she kicked constantly and flailed her hands about, grabbing hold of a stray piece of toilet paper with rapt fascination; an insatiable curiosity propelled her, as if on this very morning, after sleeping through her first night, the world was captivating. She traced her plump hand through the brown sludge that had migrated to her belly. John had to grab her fat wrist to stop her from tasting it. He'd been soiled and irritable, while she was amused and happy. "Hold *still*," he'd said harshly. She'd merely cooed. She loved him automatically, gazing up at him with unsullied devotion. Wiping her hand clean, he had looked forward to the moment when he could lay her down and take a shower. But, no. Who would hold her?

As the plane descended, she'd pursued a cry that was jagged and ongoing, almost rhythmic. He felt keenly aware of the passenger next to him, a Caribbean woman in her early fifties with an air of competence. Was she laughing at him? He would show her, and indeed he had, producing a bottle at the right moment.

He was righteous as Clara sucked silently. The woman covered her mouth with her hand, then removed it to say, "She have you tie roun' her finger." John nodded, while a surge of hostility rose in him: Sure she did—was there any other way?

In the bumpy van, the landscape grew wilder. The green dissolved, and in its place low scrubby trees and rocks erupted. Children appeared by the side of the road in navy-blue school uniforms and white socks. They carried books in their arms, across their chests. Some peered into the car with interest. A tomato-faced white man clutching a baby was all they saw, and they turned away.

The driver was headed to the east coast of the island, where the Atlantic hit the shore. The west coast, where he'd once stayed with Veronica, had the gentler Caribbean Sea, the rows of tourist hotels and attractions. It had golf, and the terrain was mellowed like green felt. The east coast, which he'd read about in the in-flight magazine, had the rougher Atlantic Ocean, surfers, rural villages in hills, wild billy goats, spindly wind-bent palm trees, pottery stands, and, apparently, just two hotels perched high on the cliffs overlooking the water. He'd chosen Lord Harrington's Castle, described as the fancier of the two, and told the driver to go there. He liked the campy, aristocratic sound of the name, the implied raggedness and grandeur. It was the sort of place Veronica would find amusing, calling it *seedy but charming*. He'd briefly considered Turtle Cove, a small but new hotel with a good package. Screw packages. He and Clara would stay at the baroque, over-the-top Lord Harrington's Castle amid billy goats and crashing waves. No doubt Veronica would find it too run down. But it was *perfect*!

There would be a perfect concentration on the given tasks without endless negotiations. John could take care of the baby, and Veronica could get some sleep. When he returned, maybe she would be feeling better.

Clara batted her little hands as they drove, as if compelled by an invisible mobile hanging before her. Her brain, her entire nervous system, had catapulted ahead in a day; her senses were clear portals opening onto a sensational world. She lunged forward as if to crawl away—she didn't even know how to sit, let alone crawl—and John had to keep pulling her back. The car accelerated up the final hill to reveal the stucco crumble that was Lord Harrington's Castle. Upon seeing it, John's chest opened as if he were returning to someplace familiar.

He'd have to call Veronica right away to let her know what had happened. One phone call and he'd be free from her new critical vision, and he'd free her from her own anxious mothering, at once overvigilant and distant. She could finally rest. Besides, he and Clara were doing fine.

But when they pulled up beside the hotel, Clara took one look at the white behemoth and started to shriek. John offered her a bottle, then the precious lamb, but she swatted them away. He was sweating and wiped his brow as Clara became frantic and twisted in his arms. Five minutes passed as the driver patiently waited to be paid and the porter came and held his backpack. Without notice, the driver gently touched Clara's back with a large hand. Startled, she stopped crying, turned to face him, then lunged for the silver hair of his beard and tugged it. Another person. A diversion. The driver took her easily into his arms and walked a few paces, leaving John both stunned and relieved. When Clara was calm, the driver placed her back in the baby carrier on John's chest, and she began to doze.

Looking around, John recognized the hotel from an old Parliament cigarette ad. The turquoise-blue sea deepened to azure behind the white pillars flanking the pool. On the beach, the impossibly tall palms bent over the powdery shore. In the foreground, two models had smoked miraculously white cigarettes. He paid the driver with dollars and gave him too large a tip. It was three P.M., and there was a strong breeze off the ocean that cooled his perspiration.

The key to his room was attached to a palm-sized brass cricket player. It knocked against the wooden door as the bellman opened it. After the ongoing preliminaries—*Would you like a beverage, sir? Do you know where is the safe?*—he would be alone with the sleeping Clara, the glass louvers smeared with sea salt. The room was compact; two double beds dominated most of it, surrounded by a thin perimeter of floor. Twin seascapes in gilt frames were hung above each bed at slightly different heights. But there was no Veronica here to finagle a better room. It would be a relief not to have to switch.

John pulled down the chenille cover on the bed and slowly placed Clara in the middle of the white sheets. Then he surrounded her with pillows. He went to the bathroom and sat down on the toilet. He made a mental note: *shower, call V.* Yes. Then he left the bathroom and lay down beside the baby. He opened his eyes, reconsidering. He didn't want to roll on top of her and possibly crush her, as Veronica always feared. She felt that co-sleeping was indulgent and didn't want Clara to get used to it. He went and lay in the other bed. He jerked awake three times to call Veronica, but he hesitated. What exactly would he say? He *had* left a note. That was good. No, he had to get up. But his lids were heavy and he would give in to sleep for just a few minutes.

He woke to the baby's cry. She looked up at him beseechingly as he stood over her bed. He undid her wet diaper and put on a fresh one. The room had grown shadier, and insects were beginning to scream. Three hours had passed. It was six in the evening. Soon Veronica would be coming home from work; she'd be worried. Two chameleons danced on the windowsill. He couldn't remember the last time he'd taken a three-hour nap. He wanted a drink before he called her. He opened the mini-fridge (old money like Veronica and her family, he'd been surprised to find, never *touched* the mini-fridge—it was too extravagant) and took out a Banks, the local beer, which tasted like freezing pennies. He'd never tasted anything as delicious. The terrazzo floor was refreshing on his hot bare feet. He picked up the phone and dialed reception to get the international code, then hung up; he would take a bath first. In the bathroom, he ran a tub and took Clara in with him. She loved the little seashell-shaped soaps and tried to eat one of them. Finished, he stepped out and wrapped a fluffy white towel—the one luxury in the room—around them both. He was good at this, he was. She was happy with him. And he knew what to do next: What to do next was food; she needed food.

He dressed and gave her the remainder of the goat-milk formula, which she chugged quickly. He would have to buy more the next day. Where would he get the herbs to go with it? The goat milk was mixed with a blend of herbs that Veronica insisted on. Regular formula she'd deemed too chemical. Clara was addicted. He wasn't sure what was in it but thought it was anise, because sometimes her breath smelled like licorice. How the hell would he get anise here? He was getting light-headed and needed to eat, so he dressed her and they left for the dining room, Clara facing forward in the carrier, kicking her legs. The evening air was incredible, warm and silky around his bare arms and neck. He heard music as he approached the dining room—brass drums and cymbals vibrating—and he smelled curry from the buffet.

He took a plate off a palm-leaf place mat and got in line with the few other people in the dining room. The hunger he felt was sharp and affirming, a proof of his vitality. He served himself some of everything, until his plate was overflowing. He was starving.

As he was walking to a table, he saw a couple, arms entwined, waiting in line. The man had long simian hands, hands he somehow knew, and the woman, who was very short, smiled at him with recognition. Joss Saperstein raised his dark eyes to John's and said, "Hey, man! What are you guys doing here?" Adele, his girlfriend, a blond Cuban, said, "Hey, I thought that was you. Veronica never told me!"

"What are *you* doing here?" John asked. His brow soaked with sweat as Joss and Adele spoke. They would tell. Joss was saying something like that now, how he *couldn't wait* to tell Art—and Art would tell Ines. Joss Saperstein was a childhood friend of Art's. John had known him for years; through Joss, Veronica had met Adele, and on occasion the two women went out. He didn't think they spoke much these days but couldn't be sure. Those were Joss's giant hands spinning on a basketball. He'd last seen him a few months ago at Ines's birthday party and enjoyed his company; John now hated Joss for being so infallibly *nice* and Adele for being so sociable.

"Where's Veronica?" Adele asked, her head tilted quizzically. "We should all have a drink together after dinner."

"She's talking to the manager about switching rooms," John said, staring straight through Adele's creamy vanilla face to some distant star. "Ours is really small." What had he done? He remembered telling Joss and Adele all about Barbados. Back at the party in the fall, it was *he* who had insisted that they come, extolling the island's many virtues with the air of an old timer, an expert.

"We'll let you go, man," Joss said, a wary but kind expression in his black brows.

John took his plate to a small table against the back wall

and unhooked Clara from his sticky chest when he sat down. Holy shit! Someone poured his water. Another person asked him if he'd like a high chair. "That would be great," he said, eager to cool off. When the high chair came, it was not the plush upholstered vinyl Italian one they had at home but a stiff wooden boxy thing with a low back. He placed Clara in it briefly, and she slumped over the edge and began to suck on the railing. He looked around, hoping no one had seen; Clara couldn't even sit up. He took her back onto his lap, smiling sheepishly when someone came and hesitantly removed the high chair. He ate fast, greedily, over her head, occasionally dropping little bits of food in her hair while she gummed a fried plantain.

"Would you like a wine list?" a server asked, as he put two glasses on the table. "Your wife is joining you?"

"Yes," he answered, he did want the wine list, but then he added, "We'll get this one," pointing to a Sancerre.

"So should I leave the place setting, sir?"

"Yes. She'll be here in a minute." When the waiter left, he shoveled his food as the baby batted at the plate, intrigued by the grains of jasmine rice that clung to her fingers.

Feeling conspicuous, he asked a busboy if he could wrap up the remainder to go. The busboy anxiously conferred with some senior person, and the two looked at John with unmasked derision. A meal was to be savored, not gobbled and carried away in haste. When had he last eaten without Veronica? It felt strange. And they never went out to dinner. They'd have to do that soon.

When the steaming sack arrived back at the table, he reattached the baby and headed for the lobby. "Is there a business center? A computer I can use?" he asked at the desk. Several slow minutes later, a lanky woman emerged and led him to a very chilly room with three ancient Dells. Each dusty mouse sat on a real linen doily, which completely prevented its ability to roll. He sat down, removed the doily, and opened his email. It had felt right to come here. He brushed some lint off the screen, considering what to say, then wrote a note to Art. He would preempt Joss Saperstein and Adele and tell Art in confidence. It had happened, the way an accident happens, but he had also done it. *Done* something. Art was more adventurous than he was. Art would appreciate it. The trip had exuberance in it, a sharp break from the quotidian. It had bravado but it was harmless. He paced the room, waiting to see if Art would send a response. After a few minutes, he heard the ping, ran to the terminal, and found the familiar subject heading: PENIS ENLARGEMENT!

He stared at the screen for a long moment, willing Art to reply, while Clara began to whimper. It was way past her bedtime; he couldn't wait much longer. He leaned forward and logged out.

In their room, he closed the door and sighed. Nothing but the Sapersteins was wrong; he'd leave the next day so he wouldn't have to worry about running into them. He ate the okra stew on the bed. Clara played with the dolphin in curry, okra with spices, tomato and shredded coconut. Veronica was testing food with the baby, giving her one taste of something at a time—bananas for three days straight to see if there was a reaction. He didn't even know if they'd graduated beyond bananas. Now Clara had licked about ten new things at once. Hoping there'd be no ill effect, John gulped his wine.

Despite the run-in, he couldn't remember a meal this

good. He offered Clara the bottle of cow's milk he'd gotten at dinner. She drank it as readily as she did her weird goat concoction. He was amazed at how easy caring for her could be when he was not constantly subject to Veronica's restrictions.

He picked up the hotel phone to call her. It was seven P.M.; no doubt she was home from work, anxious about where they were. The dial tone was loud, an anachronism in his ear. But his cell would be useless; frugality had prevented him from ever buying a global calling plan. There was a certain period of time where he could "roam" before he'd become officially out of range. He held the receiver, listening to the ringing phone, while a small but distinct hollow, the emptiness of the bereft, opened like a bubble between his lungs. Where was she?

The answering machine picked up. Shock at her absence was followed quickly by relief. He listened to the outgoing message with both of their voices and a gurgling little laugh from Clara in the background. They'd made the phone message in the fall on a monumental Sunday, the second time they'd had sex since the birth. Clara had fallen into a long nap, and Veronica was trying to take her own when John approached her. Afterward, Veronica wriggled free to go get the baby, who was "actually alive!" she'd said. She'd been nude as she held the baby and spoke into the machine. He'd always liked that message, how happy they seemed: the high-pitched cheer of Veronica's voice and that paternal deepening in his own while Clara cooed in the background. The message, the whole family, sounded perfect.

Art had once spoken of "hetero-hegemony," how "whole sections of Manhattan, once gripped by something artistic or political," were now in the throes of this instead. "Everyone's a goddamn breeder," he'd said. The four of them were in a bar downtown, and Ines had recently suffered her first miscarriage.

"Is this your way of comforting me, Art? I mean, we're try-ing. We are *trying* to breed here. That's the goal," Ines had said. Veronica had sipped her ginger ale, placing a gentle hand on her friend's shoulder. John admired and slightly envied their closeness. Ines had turned to Veronica, laughing. "Can you believe him?" John had felt a guilty but distinct satisfaction: Veronica was pregnant.

John was so moved by the sound of the message, the sound of their nuclear happiness, that he didn't flinch when her cell also went straight to voice mail. He spoke into the receiver in a voice full of warmth and distracted optimism. He didn't feel that he was being at all deceptive.

"Hey, Veronica," he began cheerfully, "hope you had a good day. We missed you this afternoon, but I thought it would be good for you to get over your cold. My mom was hot to see the baby, so we're in Irvington." He paused as the lie took hold. It was plausible. Months ago, when Veronica was recov-ering, he'd taken the baby there on several Saturdays just for the day. It was right up the Hudson, less than an hour away. He wasn't contrite but almost proud of the story's seamless feasibility, and stopped to admire it. "We're going to spend the night. Don't bother coming up. You've been sick and every-thing, and we'll probably go through some of my dad's stuff. The baby's been going down easily these days, and my mom has that Pack 'n Play we can set up. Feel better—Clara, want to say hi to Mama?" Clara breathed heavily into the receiver.

John reveled in this bit of authenticity, as if Clara's breath were proof that everything was absolutely normal. "Okay, we'll talk to you tomorrow when we figure out our train thing."

A moment later he saw a message from Veronica on his cellphone—apparently it was working—and listened to it. She was going out with Ines. Perfect. She wouldn't miss them for this one night.

Clara did go to bed easily with John holding her, a bottle tight in her hands and mouth, something Veronica never allowed. Certain books said you could not cuddle them to sleep. "They have to learn, *like we all do, to self-soothe*," Veronica had parroted. "Otherwise, the baby will wake up expecting to be cuddled throughout the night."

"Is there anything wrong with that? To expect to be held when you're a baby? If not then, when?" he'd once asked Veronica.

So John held Clara. They slept. When she stirred, he placed a big gentle hand on her belly and she was instantly quiet, her kinetic legs, her mobile face, magically stilled. Her belly rose and fell as she breathed, her tiny ribs articulated beneath his palm. The trials of the day were behind him, she was fed, bathed and he felt the satisfaction of having worked hard, possibly harder than he ever had before. He kissed the globe of her pink cheek with a mixture of gratitude (she was doing fine) and exhaustion, as a tear slid down his cheek.

He didn't know why he was crying or even the last time he had cried. It was near midnight. Nothing was wrong. His breath was calm, composed. Everything was right. The ancient music, the warmth of that yellow cab in the snow this morning, had worked like a time machine. He'd stumbled upon an open door and walked through it. He was in Barbados. The sound of the ocean soothed him. The breeze was balmy but cooler and swept through the glass louvers like a condoning hand. The Caribbean was paradise.

4

Friday

Veronica

Gliding uptown after morning rush hour, she saw the snow packed tight to the gutters, as if cleared for her. The cab sped through an unbroken chain of green lights. Despite the cold, Veronica—slightly claustrophobic in cabs—cracked both windows, savoring the chill on her face. It was disorienting, even thrilling, to be so late for work.

She pulled out her phone to look for a message from John, but there was none. She wondered if he was angry about something. Ordinarily he called back.

The extra sleep made the office, near Bryant Park, welcoming. The checked floors and frosted-glass doors made her a forties' movie star, a "career girl," with adventure awaiting. She could smell coffee, paper, and Alex's piney cologne. Alex, their twenty-six-year-old assistant, had a prominent Adam's apple and warm green eyes. His hair was a perpetually golden spot of sun. "Veronica!" he said. "We've missed you."

"I had a doctor's appointment this morning," she said, amazed that her cold was nearly gone.

Alex stood there, looking into her face for a beat too long. "Everything all right?"

"Fine," she said, as he followed her into her office with a sheaf of phone messages from the morning.

"Farmer Mendelsohn just called from New Jersey. He wants us to come up again to talk."

"Great. Did you look at the schedule?" she said with a flicker of anticipation. Mendelsohn—tall and commanding— was a raw-dairy farmer from Austria. He'd married an American, who'd conveniently inherited acres of rolling farmland that was perfect for a certain type of cow. Mendelsohn's cheese was delicious, his kitchen a bohemian paradise. The school board would never approve of disseminating his raw cheese, but Veronica was working on him, trying to get him to make a pasteurized version.

John had approved of her dairy swoon. "It's good to see you enjoying something again," he'd said one night at dinner.

"What's that supposed to mean?"

"It's just good, you loving artisanal cheese."

"What about loving Herr Mendelsohn?" Art had piped in, whereupon John and Art had begun a German-accented discussion of the merits of raw milk. The beauty of the live enzymes.

Today she did love things again. Alex stood at the edge of

her desk, staring at his laptop. "I have the train schedule here, or we could get a Zipcar," he said.

"Let's look at trains. His new hard cheeses are amazing. Murray's is going to carry them this spring." Thanks to work, the day remained buoyant, the antithesis of the tension that lately prevailed at home. She called the apartment just to see what was going on. No one answered. John must have been putting Clara to sleep. It was exhausting to continually monitor Clara's day from a distance. *After*, this was what being at work essentially meant—not being at home.

Everything was fine. But throughout the day she fumed each time she looked at her phone and saw that John hadn't called. Mendelsohn was also silent, each man amplifying the absence of the other. At noon she spoke, unsatisfactorily, with Jamie, Mendelsohn's overburdened wife.

"Al's milking," she told Veronica disconsolately. "I actually *don't* think he can call you back today." Jamie protected Al's time as if he were an artist at work.

"Do you know when he can call me, Jamie? Do you think tomorrow?" She scrolled through her contacts list to see if she had a cell number for Al, if she could bypass Jamie and call him directly.

"Tomorrow one of our cows will be birthing," Jamie said flatly.

"The school board is giving us dispensation to choose the farmers we like for Jasper. We have a deadline. It would be great if you would let Al know we called and we're definitely interested in coming back."

"You guys are coming back here?" Jamie was averse to business of any kind—a trait Veronica's father had, mistak-

enly, assigned to her. Compared with Jamie, she was a captain
of industry.

The day swirled busily around her. Hours passed in calls
with Sanitation, which still hadn't removed the empty vending machines from Jasper. She had several calls with the prin-
cipal of Jasper as they tried to determine who would pay for
the removal. At two o'clock she stretched, realizing she hadn't
eaten lunch. She was about to get up when a bubble floated
across her screen.

HI, GORGEOUS.

The sender was Damon King. He was her last boyfriend,
the boyfriend right before she'd met John a decade ago. He'd
crushed her thoroughly with his erratic affection and his eva-
sions. Damon, peripatetic but indelible. He was a talented
photojournalist, so willowy he was nearly feminine, but with
a rugged resemblance to Clint Eastwood. Over the years, he'd
pop into town and invite her to coffee. She always agreed to
meet him, as if to ascertain once and for all whether or not
he'd loved her. But he was consistently so flattering that she
could never be sure. Why had she needed to know? She watched
the message bubble glide to the corner of her screen. By *not*
knowing, she had her answer: He had not loved her. Still, the
painful impossibility of union sustained his glamour.

As she pushed herself away from her desk, another bubble
popped up.

I'M IN NY.

She hadn't seen him in three years. At their last meeting,
he'd been asking her about John's name, if it was spelled with
an *h* or was it "short for Jonathan," when he'd leaned across
the table and kissed her. They were at a Middle Eastern place

on Avenue A, and the whole room, the green glasses and little oily plates of black olives, vanished into a timeless crevasse for a long, sea-deep moment. Opening her eyes, she realized she'd dipped her elbow in the hummus. Wiping it off furiously with a wet napkin, she felt the tidal pull, the force of his desire, and the sickening certainty of her own. She'd thrown down some bills, flown from her seat, and run all the way home, sweating by the time she reached the loft. They hadn't spoken since.

She vowed to ignore him when another chime sounded: DINNER AT ISABELLA'S TOMORROW, he wrote. He was so confident of his power over her that he didn't even put a question mark after his message. His huge arrogance was almost funny. He *was* funny. And a good kisser. She stopped. She popped his bubble with a single click and went to lunch.

By the end of the day, John still hadn't called. What could the two of them be *doing*? Crawling into a tent at Paragon? Tasting samples of Spanish sherry at the new liquor store on Broadway? It infuriated her not to know. Again, she reached his voice mail.

"Hi. Where *are* you guys? I'm assuming you went for a walk this morning. Maybe you turned off the ringer while she napped. . . . Anyway, please call me. I won't be straight home after work, if that's all right with you. I haven't seen Ines in ages. They're pregnant again, so we're sort of celebrating. Kiss Clara for me." The phone felt hollow in her palm, eerily light; it had been too easy to free herself.

She pictured Clara rolling on the fleece rug. The baby had

just started giggling too, real belly laughs that seemed to arrive at the right instant.

She examined her reflection in the mirror of a small compact she kept in her desk. From the other room, Alex saw her and quickly looked away. Her eyes were bright and clear, her lips dark even without lipstick. She dabbed a little Orgasm on her cheeks. She looked okay, and it was a shame John wouldn't see her this way. She and Ines had always thought that if you looked all right you needed to seize the moment. (Without notice, you could look pale and ancient and rush online to research symptoms of rare illnesses.)

Looking up from her desk, she saw Alex hesitating in the vestibule, holding the elevator open for her. Everyone else had left for the day. "Are you walking to the train?" he asked with undeniable hope. She left her office and joined him. In the elevator he ventured, "You seem distracted—the cheese farmer?"

"Oh yeah! Whatever. Can you imagine being that flaky? Not calling back all day when this could be a big opportunity for him?" She wasn't thinking of Mendelsohn but of John. They pushed through the doors to a street so dark it looked like it had never been day.

"He's got to ditch the wife," Alex said, trying to bond with Veronica but merely exhibiting his youth: Mendelsohn and his wife had three blond children under age four. He couldn't simply excise his wife. She felt an affectionate impulse to shield Alex from these complications.

"Heading home?" he asked as they headed underground to the subway.

"Yup," she lied. It would mean she could get on a different

train from Alex, whose overfamiliarity was starting to feel awkward. "Clara's waiting for me," she added, and to make her goodbye final she reached up to him on tiptoe—he was quite gangly—and gave him a peck on his cheek. She felt him freeze beneath her touch and then stare at her in mute wonder as she turned and walked toward her own platform.

What was *that*? Something new, an aura, seemed to surround her. It went beyond the extra sleep—perhaps it was the new cocktail of pills—a blast of nerve endings opening. On the ride up to 72nd Street, she felt men stare at her and glance away. It was Friday night and the trains were packed. She could smell bodies. The tang of sweat through wool. Where was everyone going? She and John went out seldom now, and it was exciting to be alone on the train.

Walking up West End Avenue, Veronica laughed at the sudden majesty of the homey street. She'd never noticed the glamour of the art deco buildings. She was free, yet a sharp longing lingered; she hadn't seen Clara for nearly twenty-four hours. She'd derided John for getting up to check on her, when it was actually kind of sweet. Why had she not wanted to stare at her sleeping child? Now just a glimpse of the baby would settle the fluttering in her gut.

Her phone vibrated and a message light appeared. John had called while she was on the train. She stopped walking to listen to his message.

"Hey, Veronica, hope you had a good day. We missed you this afternoon, but I thought it would be good for you to get over your cold. My mom was hot to see the baby, so we're in Irvington."

She paused it and replayed it from the beginning; he'd taken

Clara to his mother's a few times when she'd been recovering but never without consulting her. She listened as one would to a film in a foreign language studied long ago. He hesitated after he said the word *Irvington*. Then—and this was sort of unbelievable—he told her not to come.

She had to come. They were always offering each other breaks from child care, which neither person accepted. It was an unofficial rule of conduct between them. But an unplanned trip was unprecedented—he'd never done *anything* with the baby without first asking Veronica. *"Feel better—Clara, want to say hi to Mama?"* Clara panted a bit, which made Veronica smile broadly and for the moment made everything seem ordinary. *"Okay, we'll talk to you tomorrow when we figure out our train thing."*

Odd. But perhaps it was also ideal. Her own guilt was absolved. The baby was in love with her grandmother. If they were gone, they wouldn't miss her at home for one evening.

The wind picked up as she leaned against the building to call Irvington. A loathsome busy signal greeted her. John's mother, Muriel, had never adapted to call-waiting. Veronica hung up and punched the call in again. She kept calling until her fingers were numb. Tears of frustration stung her eyes. A block away, she saw Ines's warm awning. Muriel remained enchanted by a conversation with someone.

Ines answered the door, wearing a tight cobalt-blue dress. Her black hair was thicker, frizzier around her face, and the whites of her eyes shone. She looked striking but older. That was how it was these days seeing Ines, the barometer of Veronica's own life. Ines, who had once been a teenager in a vintage dress with a creaseless marble face. They were changing.

"I thought you were Art," Ines said, her disappointment obvious. "What's wrong?"

"Nothing. Are you okay?"

Ines held a piece of blue carbon paper in her hand and waved it at Veronica. "I got this weird test result. I just had it done, for the nuchal translucency, and there was something off, a number that was close to the border, they said."

Veronica took off her black wool coat and laid it on a chair. "The border of what?"

Ines paced, her bare feet clenching the parquet floor. "The number they're looking for. The number that's normal. They want a two-point-oh at eleven weeks and I have a two-point-six. Art doesn't know yet. He's flying. He should be home any minute, though."

Veronica followed Ines into the kitchen. "Where'd he go?" she asked.

"He's in Des Moines, Iowa, for a happiness-studies conference." Art, an unpublished academic, was an adjunct lecturer of anthropology for the tenth year in a row. He was not ambitious, but he was happy, and he was studying happiness.

"Des Moines? How could you be happy there?"

"Exactly. Anyway, I'm supposed to get retested on Monday. I have to wait all weekend. It's agony."

"It'll be fine." She believed it. With someone else's trouble it was easier to believe it would be fine. "I'm so thrilled for you. Here." Veronica unveiled a bouquet of wind-beaten red tulips, and Ines took them and started to search for a vase.

"If the result still isn't what they want, they'll retest again next week, just to see—" She stopped speaking and started to cry quietly into a cupped hand.

"Oh dear." They hugged, the full length of their bodies pressed together.

"This is all really stressful," Ines said, "it finally happening and then not knowing—" Ines was a believer in unambiguous answers, clear test results. She was the salve, the one with finite answers for Veronica's constant wavering. Ines pulled away to gain composure. She blew her nose heartily on a dish towel. "I wish I could drink with you. Here," she said, handing Veronica a bottle of red to open. Veronica poured a small glass and toasted Ines.

"Congratulations."

"Thank you. I'm cautiously optimistic, but we'll see." Ines turned and began peeling a clove of garlic.

"Two-point-six doesn't sound far off at all." But Veronica knew it could be. The numbers could be dreadfully wrong. Veronica's amniotic fluid had been too low: four-point-something when it was supposed to be at least five. Two-point-six, whatever that meant, could be *terrible*. "How's Art doing? He must be ecstatic."

Ines sat down at the table across from her. "He is—my God, he's so happy he's speaking with a Long Island accent! You know how he does that when he's excited?"

"I do." Outside, it had started to snow again. The lights of the avenue blurred in the purple evening. She wanted to fly right out into it, link arms with Ines, and go drink hot sake around the corner. "You shouldn't cook. Let's go out instead. It'll be easier. What do you think?"

"It's just that Arthur . . . He should be here any second, then we could leave. I need to talk to him first."

"Call him."

"He's in transit. Anyway, where's John?"

"In Irvington, *with Clara*, actually. He let me sleep in this morning and then left this cryptic note—I haven't heard from them all day. I may have to go up there tomorrow."

"How will you get Muriel to stop?" Ines said. John's mother was a lanky former kindergarten teacher in her sixties, who "loved" public radio and always spoke to Veronica in a hushed voice of her many miscarriages between her two children. Muriel was trying to connect with Veronica, but Veronica, raised to keep her chin up, was embarrassed by her frankness.

"Usually Muriel stops talking about *the trials of women of reproductive age* when we focus on Clara. She'll be so involved with the baby, it will be *fine*. But what's weird is that John didn't even talk to me about this." Veronica pulled open the fridge and peered into it. She lifted a jar of giant capers and examined the label. For a moment she wished she'd called Adele, who was childless and always going out.

"Huh? You all right?"

"Yes. No. I've had this amazing energy today. I'm taking these new meds, which might be starting to work." A new energy presided, but it was shaky, shifting. "Maybe it's hormonal, I don't know. . . . Sometimes I wish we could just disappear in the dark auditorium, watching slides of Giottos. . . . I just want—"

Ines smiled at the memory. Art history their freshman year. With Ines next to her in that dark room, Veronica had savored Giotto's blues. The pigments made with egg yolk and their incredible longevity, a revolutionary nuance in expression and gesture. Ines, too, understood the miracle of those colors. They'd become art lovers together. Now they were mothers.

She felt Ines's steady gaze, the clear, direct vision of her friend who never looked away. Damon! Adele! These undeniably exciting people who had nothing to do with her current life were populating her mind; they came like djinnis, smiling, offering. *Here's a message from the outside world,* they seemed to say. There was Adele's gallery on 25th Street and Damon in war-torn places, photographing Taliban. The world was big and affecting. Where had she been? Inside a cocoon. "See, I wish I missed John, but I don't." Instead, she thought of the true hurt in Damon's gray eyes as she'd run from the café.

"You do miss him. Go to Irvington. Muriel can watch the baby, and you and John can go out on a date."

"A date!" When she was alone with John, he often looked into her eyes with some unspoken question that she never had the answer to. She wasn't even sure what the question was. She imagined his curly light-brown hair—cut like a benevolent Caesar—with a pang of nostalgia.

"Come, my love," Ines said. "We'll eat." Ines was tossing a salad and had put on water for the pasta.

"Really, with your partner a day is not long, but with your child, you'll see, it's an eternity. You sort of shore yourself up when you have to be apart, steel yourself, and just get busy, but you still miss her." How could she go on to the newly pregnant Ines about missing her child?

"Go, then," Ines said, with a note of impatience.

"You're probably right," Veronica said, disturbed by John's

seeming indifference to her. At one point in their lives, each parting had been fraught. He used to run uptown to reunite with her after basketball games and would arrive panting, sweat falling in fat drops to the floor. She'd embraced him, inhaling every wet, salty pore. That desperation to connect was gone.

"Where the hell is Art? His plane was supposed to have landed by now."

The small galley kitchen grew unbearably hot. Veronica peeled off her thin black sweater and sat down, holding the edge of the table. Her heart rate seemed to catapult ahead of her, some lone *part* galloping on the loose. "At the same time, while John's gone, I want to do everything I can't do when he's here, like—" She paused. Whole chunks of vocabulary had been engulfed by months of exhaustion. "Like not always reading in bed. Like saying I don't want to read my book, I want to sleep."

"Like fucking?" Ines said. A pan sizzled on the stove. A smell like sautéed earth filled the room. Ines's eyes danced with mischief. She moved to get the pasta. She was a goddess with steam from the colander enveloping her in her blue dress and electric hair. Once, when they were drunk, she and Veronica had kissed. They'd been seeing these pompous men from Harvard, and it had been the most comforting and affirming kiss. A real French kiss in the bathroom of a bar in Cambridge. They'd never spoken about it, but Veronica was immune all evening as her date flirted with other women.

Sweat beaded above her lip. John's distance pierced her.

"Well, you can't sleep with John when he's not here," Ines added.

"No, I suppose that's true," Veronica said gravely.

"Fine, go to Irvington. Or *don't* go to Irvington. Absence makes the heart grow fonder. Stay in the city with me and Art."

"Whose heart will grow fonder?" she asked.

"Well, both of your hearts, V." In the hush of steam, high up on the seventeenth floor with the slim window view of the alleyway, they were just two women standing in a kitchen, about to eat pasta. Veronica was a tiny speck in a vast universe; she was nothing, but in a good way she had learned in college, in a class called Philosophy of Religion. You were everything to yourself, but then, when seen from a certain, non-disparaging angle, you were of equal value as an armrest, a carpet, or a plant. She was composed only of matter.

As she sat down to eat, the speck-in-the-universe feeling evaporated. She thought of Clara and the goat milk she needed to pick up on her way to Irvington. There was no way he'd brought enough. Everything was important again. Ines would know this soon, the ever-present vigilance. "So, what's happened so far? The seven-week sono, right, and yesterday's test . . ."

"It still seems distant, you know, that this will actually continue and I'll have a baby."

Veronica squeezed Ines's hand, wishing she could banish her friend's fear.

"The next test is the triple screen, then CVS or amnio," Ines said.

"It's a nightmare."

"It's not a nightmare for me. I love it. It's like collecting peace of mind, insurance with each test. I only need the result of this one. . . ." Ines had become an underwriter for an insurance company. She had given up editing independent film forever for something dependable.

"And you like your OB, right?" Veronica asked. "That's really important too."

"I do."

"Are you going to consider the birthing center instead of the hospital? There are so many interventions, so many unnecessary things they do to you in the hospital."

"*Unnecessary?* Veronica, they saved your life. And Clara's too. Thank God you weren't stuck at the birthing center."

"It's just that at the birthing center they don't induce." On Veronica's due date, nothing had happened. Her cervical dilation was zero. "There's this chain reaction. The low amniotic fluid led to the induction with Pitocin, which led to the bleeding—" She was blathering to ecstatic Ines about her difficult labor. She had to stop herself.

"I *want* the epidural," Ines snapped.

"I want you to have a better experience than I did." She sipped her wine. "And chances are you will." Veronica had signed and faxed all the right forms, but the doctor's office still wouldn't send her a copy of Clara's birth record. There was a sequence of events she was trying to understand. She was sliding back into that story.

"It was modern medicine. It wasn't anyone's fault."

"I keep wondering if the fluid was really *that* low, if some variable had changed . . ." She looked into her wineglass and drained it.

"You had nothing to do with what happened, and you have Clara," Ines assured her. "I *want* interventions. The more medicated, the better. We're different," Ines said, wiping the corners of her mouth. "What's one thing for you is another for me, and I can handle it."

Veronica put down her fork. "You can handle it? Do you think I haven't handled it?"

"No—only that you obsess. And you're *fine*."

"I'm sorry," she said, choked. "I know I've been very preoccupied." She had been too preoccupied to know early on about Ines's pregnancy, too selfish to have been a confidante.

"Let's let it go," Ines said. They ate silently. Ines paused to check her computer. "He landed."

"They should've had the conference someplace actually hedonic—just for fun. If they're going to study happiness, they should know what it feels like."

"They should've met in Barbados," Ines said.

"Yes! I remember seeing this orchid cave there when I was ten—the most amazing *natural* colors. And the *air*. The tactile air." She smiled, remembering John there too, on her annual family trip when they were just twenty-five, sneaking into her room with a red hibiscus, cracking open some aloe stems, and cooling her sunburned shoulders.

"At ten, did you rhapsodize about the air?"

"You know I did." She poured herself an inch more of wine. What was life about if not pleasure? She picked an errant strand of linguine off her place mat and ate it.

"Look at you," Ines said, gesturing to Veronica's empty plate. It was as if they were both reminded of the sensual Veronica of *before*. Fleetingly, with linguine and the very word *Barbados*, she'd returned.

"I could murder him," Ines said. "Look, he leaves his crack-berry here on the counter. He hasn't even been getting my emails. He lives in another century, I swear."

In the lobby, Veronica bumped into Art coming home. Lost in thought, he brightened when he saw her.

"Art! How was the conference? Are you happy?"

"Hey!" He hugged her firmly, a liberty he took with his wife's best friend. "I *am* happy, even though commuting is the opposite of sex—in terms of reported happiness levels."

"It's not like you have to *commute* to Des Moines and back."

"Where's John?"

"In Irvington with the baby."

"And you're at my house, drinking my Barolo with my pregnant wife. Is there any left?"

"I didn't polish it off by myself! Congratulations, by the way."

"I'm a stud, I know." Arthur was just five foot seven and had a large mop of black hair, a slight paunch, and an overall troll-like look. She adored him. They stood there appraising each other.

"We need to have dinner with you guys, the four of us, *soon*," she said. John had told her ages ago that Art found her regal and intimidating, and she liked it, standing there feeling statuesque in his gaze.

"Definitely. Your husband has been hard to pin down lately."

"I've been trying to reach him all day." Beneath her smile, a shadow flapped vigorously. Pain gripped her abdomen tightly, then released. Yes, a whole day had passed.

"Ah, the elusive John Reed."

Veronica and Art parted with another tight hug. She felt as if he'd dusted her with something, replaced apprehension with joy.

Outside she huddled under a Gray's Papaya awning to check her phone before getting on the train. Nothing. She called John's cell and it went immediately to voice mail. She ducked down into the ground, to the roar and heat of the trains, tempted to throw the phone beneath one.

So he had gone. The fast ride was liberating, the smooth seat of the new train carrying her effortlessly on a silky ribbon of track. Through the inky dark and intermittent flashes of light she flew.

At home, there were no messages. Not even Damon's ludicrous bubbles appeared. She considered calling Irvington again, but it was late; she didn't want to wake Muriel. She sighed at the medicinal whiteness of the kitchen, the spare lines of a reclaimed-wood dining table anchored with a bowl of untouched French sea salt. In the master bedroom, the huge wall of built-in closets seemed excessive.

She ran a hot bath and submerged herself all the way, feeling the water trickle onto her scalp. Surfacing, she squeezed and released Clara's purple rubber duck. He could at least call to say good night.

When she got out, she found herself sweating in her robe, staring at Clara's empty crib. She sat down in the suede glider, the fleece rug plush between her toes, and stared at a framed poster of Celeste, the elephant queen, which hung above the changing table. A Calder mobile made its slow turn above the crib. It was an ideal nursery. Still warm from the bath, she wandered into the kitchen and opened the freezer, where she found John's ice cream, two-thirds of a pint of Chubby Hubby. Digging in, she felt the fat and sugar coat her tongue and settle warmly in her belly as she read the label, checking it for artificial gums and fillers. She couldn't remember the last time she'd even had ice cream. She summoned Ines's words—*it's one night*—and ate some more. John really was kind to go away with the baby and give her this break.

Nude in bed, she touched herself. She was never alone anymore. Her own wetness came as a surprise, as if she lay there with a double. But, no, it was *her*. Something was recalibrating. Maybe it had begun that morning, the extra sleep seeping through her like flour through a sieve. All at once she was thinking he'd be faceless, whoever he was, but with massive hands and a tight ass, grinding into her. All at once, she was coming. She lay in the center of the bed and smiled as she fell happily away into Saturday.

5

Saturday

John

What blooms in the dark? John forgot the name of it, but all
night long he dreamed of the white flower. Its heady scent was
reminiscent of April in New York, when all the trees are bud-
ding with popcorn and all the people are in love. He didn't
know when he'd last felt this giddy, this free of heartbreak;
he'd been heartbroken since the birth, living with this Veronica of *after*, almost mourning. He remembered the name of
that flower—*frangipani*. On the way back to the room, he'd
overheard the concierge in the mint-green slacks talking about
it to a shy, uninterested teenage girl. When he'd finally cleared
the bits of okra stew off the bed and began to doze, he thought
he smelled it coming in the window like a ghost of honey.

John woke feeling sticky. He sat up to check on Clara. She
looked as if a vanilla milk shake had been spilled over her chin
and chest. The once-fragrant air smelled sour. He watched

helplessly as her tiny body heaved and more of the white substance oozed out of her mouth. A sickening doom filled his chest. She could not be ill. He could not fail. He sat the wobbly baby upright and tried to wipe her off with the sheets. Her sweet head lolled to one side with exhaustion. Her head seemed so large on her neck, like a cantaloupe on a thread.

It must have been the cow milk from last night. He remembered Ines and Veronica speaking with authority about the horrors of cow milk, how it was the hardest milk to digest. Formula, they decreed, was even worse. It was an idea that implied that what they—all four of them—had consumed as infants was not good enough. Arthur and John had merely glanced at each other to note their shared resignation.

Now John was alone with Clara and she was sick from cow milk. He picked up her small, lightly trembling body. He'd never seen her this sick. Her limbs were frail as kindling in his arms. He undressed her, placed a thick towel in the sink, and laid her in it. He rinsed her skin with handfuls of warm water. "Dada," she said mournfully. Her skin was silken, and she looked up at him with a tight line of energy that implored him to stay with her, to help her. When Clara was clean, he wrapped her in a fresh towel and held her close to stop her trembling. Her cheek was fiery against his. In the diaper bag, he found the pink liquid medicine, filled the dropper, and gave her a dose. Veronica had insisted they keep some Tylenol in the diaper bag. Alone, he could see that she often knew best.

Frangipani was Veronica's flower. The one time they'd been here together, she snapped a blossom from the tree and tucked it into her bun. Later, when she left his bed—for they were unmarried, guests of her parents, and not permitted to share one—he'd found the flower bruised and damp against the white sheet.

At the breakfast buffet, he wore his dark glasses and stepped into line. They had to have goat milk; there were goats surrounding this place. He gave Clara some papaya, which Veronica had told him was good for digestion, and she ate it off his fingers hungrily. A good sign, he thought. Then he went to the cereal buffet with Clara on his hip. "Do you have goat milk, by any chance?" he asked a server.

The man smiled at John and said, "Cow milk here, sir."

"I know, but do you also have any goat milk? Or do you know where I can get some?" A beam of sun cast prisms on the glass pitchers between them.

"We don't have goat milk, sir." In that bright surreal moment, two goats walked by just behind the breakfast pavilion and brayed.

"You've got to. I mean, look!" John laughed, pointing, but the server remained impassive. Clara was batting at the light, trying to lean over and out of her father's arms to touch it or some other evanescent but fascinating thing.

"I understand your request, sir, but we don't have goat milk."

"Someone has to have it, somewhere. It's for the baby." Clara lunged almost out of his arms, and he let her grab a piece of butter in golden fail, stacked in a bowl of ice.

"Let me get the manager for you, sir. Maybe she can be of assistance." The server walked off very slowly, leaving the cow milk sweating in an iced pitcher, where a fly darted around the rim. Clara's fever seemed to be lifting, and she kicked her legs with delight when John pointed at the goats. She squeezed the pat of butter and it began to melt in her fist.

"Dadoodoo dadooo daddooo da!" she said.

John was thrilled. She didn't know what she was saying, but one day—and they were getting nearer to it—she would call him Daddy. "Did you say Daddy?"

"Dadooooooo!" she said, while a long string of spit stretched from her chin.

He took her back to their table, and they spoke and smiled at each other.

"Dadooo," she said.

"Daddy."

"Dadooo."

"Say *Daddy*."

"Dadoooooooo."

"Close enough."

The drug had worked. Within twenty minutes she'd recovered. Her babbling restored his confidence. When the manager finally arrived, it felt like an interruption. She stood before him, very erect, with a regal forehead and a scent of talcum powder.

"Hello, Mr. Reed?" she said.

"Dadoo," he finished saying to Clara, and then addressed the manager. "Oh, hello."

"How may I help you today?"

"I was looking for goat milk for my daughter. That's what she drinks."

"I'm sorry we don't provide that, Mr. Reed, but we do provide cow milk. May I go get some for you, put it in her bottle?" She reached for the bottle with elegant brown fingers.

"I think cow milk makes her sick. But there are goats—I mean, if you could tell me how to get to the town, to a store, a grocery store."

She looked amused and folded her arms over her chest as if that were an impossible proposition. "That is a very uncommon request. We strive to give you all you need here at the hotel, all the best foods that we have flown in."

It was absurd to fly food in to a place where you could grow anything. "Okay, but if I needed to get some—"

"We don't get everything here in our stores. We *import*. I will get the concierge for you, sir. Maybe he can help you with your shopping."

"I don't want to shop," he said to Clara once the manager left. She looked at him with total understanding and cooed. He watched as the manager stopped at the cereal bar. She poured some milk into a small glass and sniffed it.

Clara seemed to have completely recovered. Maybe it wasn't the milk. Maybe it was something in that okra stew. He did not want Ines and Veronica to be right, and because Clara needed a bottle—she was grabbing the empty thing and tilting it to her lips—he went to the cereal bar and poured cow milk in her bottle. She dove at it and consumed it all quickly. He didn't want to believe it was not simple. The baby is hungry; you feed her.

John was trying to justify what he'd just done when the concierge appeared. He was wearing the same mint-green slacks, and his skin was very dark. "I see she satisfied now?"

"Yes, she's all right," he said, slightly embarrassed. "Thank you." None of this, he told himself, was rocket science.

On the way back to their room, he stopped in the lobby to visit the business center. He immediately found several e-mails from Caroline, the administrator at Miller Equities. *Miller Equities*, he mouthed to himself. *I'm a grown-up. I work at a company*. It seemed funnier to him than anything he could imagine. He had been a boy, chasing a squirrel over the fall leaves until it ran into a muffler. How did he get here? He'd look at the work emails later: He'd been out only one day. He scanned the list for a message from Arthur Greene, but there was none. After a dull ping, Art's message appeared on top. There was no subject heading.

John opened it to find a single word: WHAT?

He hovered there, his fingers poised over the keys. He despised Art's use of all caps. It felt like an indictment. But how could he reply? He was so far away. Through the window he saw the ocean glinting in the already high sun. They had to go swimming, once, at least. Then they'd leave.

In the room, he packed up their few belongings and busied himself for the beach, which he'd been dreaming about since they boarded the plane at Kennedy. He slathered some lotion he found in a basket in the bathroom on his pale chest and nose and all over Clara. He wanted his father to know that he'd protected her. This was something he did: conjured his dead dad at certain moments to show him his competence.

Evan Reed, good liberal and good father, was watching, not *scrutinizing*, as Veronica had once characterized it. His father had been a mid-level executive in medical publishing. It was "lucrative," Evan used to say, "but not *obscene*." No, his parents felt that obscenity was John's realm. It was laughable; aside from the support staff he was probably the least well-paid person at Miller Equities. That said, he made almost six times what he'd earned at the *Journal*. He was the quiet one in the firm, gathering information behind the scenes; he effected change but never made a decision. "I'm *so* not a big shot," he'd told them. "Great if I were, but I'm not by any stretch!" Evan had obstinately misunderstood this as false modesty, and Muriel liked her son better as a writer.

John recalled the awkward announcement that he and Veronica had made as they sat around a scarred thirty-year-old picnic table in Irvington. "*The Wall Street Journal* is nothing to sneeze at," Evan had said. "You're a writer, not a *money* guy." Muriel gazed down at a dish of stuffed grape leaves and covered her mouth with both hands.

"What, Mom? Just say what you want, okay?"

"Nothing, honey." Muriel's voice shook a little, as it always did, as it moved syllable by syllable with cautious intention. "It's just that your father and I think that, well, in terms of *contributing*—"

"I'm writing about big pharm!"

His parents exchanged a private look, after which Muriel was encouraged. They had the kind of marriage that people admired, that in its exclusivity made their *kids* almost envious. John and his sister, Sasha, felt they could never live up to it. Even in the glowy time between Veronica and John, his parents regarded them with patronizing distraction. It was as if he and Veronica were acting at being in love, were trying it on. Muriel and Evan were so *sincere,* so very authentic, that everything around them was diminished.

"We just think you write so well," Muriel said, "and you could write about other things too, you know."

Their approval had escaped him. Maybe Evan could finally appreciate John now that he'd become a father, now that he was doing something, fathering, that was irrefutably *good*.

But Evan had never known John as a father. He died of a heart attack when Veronica was pregnant. He'd had no prior history of heart trouble, and most of what he published was about coronary disease; John and Muriel had once confessed their shared magical belief that this particular area of Evan's knowledge should have made a heart attack impossible.

John adjusted Clara so her nose wasn't smashed against the cloth of the BabyBjörn. There was always the fear of suffocation. Maybe Evan died because John decided to make money instead of write about it (or at least that was the way that Evan phrased it, and he wasn't entirely wrong). There was an unspoken conceit; John knew from observing Veronica's father that the rich thought they'd become rich because they were smarter, when actually they were rich because they'd aimed for money all along. They weren't more gifted; it was what they *chose*.

At thirty-one John *chose*, feeling both his father's antipathy and Veronica's father's approbation. Soon Veronica would become pregnant. She worked for a nonprofit, and John was writing. His prestigious bylines buoyed him for a few days but never seemed to cause a strike at Pfizer or stir any publisher's interest in a book deal. And life was expensive. Veronica wouldn't admit it, but she was accustomed to luxury—a certain type of Italian sheet that was very soft but ripped easily, fresh flowers when she felt like them, all her food from locally sourced organic farms, and cabs—and he didn't want to be beholden to her father, asking for loans he could never repay. John had to review all this regularly in his mind, to legitimize it, as he did now, even while on vacation.

Vacation? Evan would say. John shrugged in defiance. And why not? He'd been on a treadmill since Clara was born; he was running to finish his work, to get home, to have a few minutes with the baby before she slept, to elicit some spark from his stony wife, to breathe. And then he did it all over again, day after day. He'd sorely needed a vacation.

On the jagged rock steps that cleaved to the side of a cliff, holding Clara tight to his chest with one hand as the other grasped on to the prickly rope banister, he was almost content. Evan, like Joss Saperstein's girlfriend, Adele, would wonder, *Where's Veronica?* A simple enough question. John looked toward the hotel, where she would be getting dressed. John would remind Evan about sunscreen and that funny mole on her chest. Evan would nod, because he knew the literature on melanoma.

There had been little time to grieve Evan; there had been only the future. Even on the day of the funeral, John had buried his face in Veronica's shoulder and embraced a body that seemed to be leavening like warm bread. She'd pulled his hand to her belly to feel a kick that was forceful, adamant.

Reaching the beach, he saw men setting up royal-blue umbrellas in the sand. It wasn't the nicest hotel in the world, but it was *trying,* and its guests who wore heels on the beach and ordered Chablis were trying too.

He was thirsty and flagged down a waiter—waiters on the beach! They'd never condone such decadence in Irvington. A waiter stood before him, perspiring in his uniform. "I'll have a . . . uh . . . a piña colada. How's that?"

"That's fine, sir."

John had considered saying the word *virgin*—it was barely ten A.M. and he hadn't slept much in the past day or longer—but he needed his mind to stop. Plus, he'd missed Friday's morning meeting with the principals at Miller Equities. Yes, he'd emailed his report on Lancelot Drugs, but it was too sketchy, almost threadbare, and Lloyd Miller, who was very old school, was most likely pissed at having to make do without hard copies. Miller was the same age as John but, because he was John's boss, because he always appeared in a suit with an ironed handkerchief, he seemed older. John spread a towel on the sand, then released Clara from the Björn, placing her in the shade of a large palm. Veronica would approve.

"Here's your drink, sir," the waiter said, setting it down on a tray next to a plate stacked with Pringles. For a moment John's panic ceased.

He looked out at the ocean. The waves curled in large turquoise tunnels, and a few, far out, were dotted with surfers. Nearby, two pale hotel guests lay on their towels like beached seals, and behind him, under the tree, a man with dreadlocks was hacking open a coconut with a pocketknife. John felt lucky again, elated to be among such beauty and warmth. *Call Muriel, call Veronica,* he told himself. Veronica wouldn't want to go to Irvington—she found his well-meaning mother annoying. By mentioning Irvington in his phone message, he had bought a little more time.

Behind him he could hear the effort of the man opening

the coconut. Clara slept soundly. She looked peaceful. He rested for a moment, watching her.

The man with the coconut walked past, offering a large chunk of the white meat to a woman in massive sunglasses. The woman shook her head and adjusted her chair so her back was to him. When the man turned around, John caught his eye. He squatted down before John with the dripping husk. "Do you want to taste this for three Beewee?" he asked.

"I can give you a dollar. I haven't had time to change currency."

"Sorry to bother you while you relax. This is a very good coconut, though. You should try it."

John took a piece and bit into it. It crunched and filled his mouth with unexpectedly sweet water. It was unbelievably good.

"Would you like some more, like to buy the rest?"

"Sure," John said, feeling magnanimous and handing him five dollars.

The man pocketed it slowly, trying not to appear needy. "I used to sell my pottery on the beach, but the hotel cracked down and doesn't allow it anymore. People get offended," he said, looking toward the woman who had turned her back to him.

"American women get easily offended," John said.

The man laughed. "I'm Derek," he said, and shook John's hand. "You married to one, her mother?" he asked, gesturing toward the baby.

"I am, and she hates buying things on the beach, I can assure you."

Derek laughed. They talked for a while. He'd gone to university in the States for a year and claimed to know all about American women. He came back to the island when his mother was dying. "Then I fell in love, got stuck here," he said, blushing. "In a few months we're moving to London."

"People always want to leave home—even places like this. This beautiful. I mean, you get to *live* here."

"But there's no work here, except in tourism. I can't—the uniforms . . ." He trailed off. "New York would be exceptionally cool!"

"You'd think," John said, remembering the constriction that would grip his throat as he stood in line at Duane Reade buying diapers, or as he made his way through packs of tourists snapping photos with their cellphones on Houston Street. The total lack of imagination in their repetitive evenings at the same places. Isabella's for dinner again. What was so great about that?

Clara woke up with a few little grunts and a huge stretch. John scooped her up and then noticed the odor of her diaper. Derek smiled at the baby and offered her a finger to squeeze.

"Thank you, this is good," John said, gesturing with the coconut.

Derek waved goodbye with a long brown hand. "Take care, New Yorker," he said.

John looked up at the steep, vine-covered steps that led back to the hotel and decided to change Clara here at the beach.

"Hey, wait," John called out suddenly to Derek.

Derek returned and crouched down to face him. His body emitted the strong odor of sex. "You want something else? You smoke?" Derek asked.

"No. I do have a question, though. Do you know where the nearest grocery store is?"

"It's not exactly a grocery store. Not a supermarket but a small store," he said. He wore a close-fitting green T-shirt and tight black trunks. Juice from the coconut dripped from his fingers. "I'll show you," he said, "if you have time."

"That would be great. I need to get some things." John gathered Clara's tiny ankles in one hand and wiped her clean with the other, careful to do so in the right direction.

"What's her name?" Derek asked.

"Oh, this is Clara."

"She's beautiful," he said. "You can follow me when you're ready."

When John was done, he followed Derek up over the small dunes and into a red Toyota Corolla that smelled like pot and ripe bananas. There were no seat belts. Derek quickly wiped sand off the seats. When John was settled and the door shut, Derek offered him a joint.

"Thanks," John said, surprised by his own failure to hesitate. He usually claimed to dislike pot, or rather the laxity of spirit it seemed to produce. Derek lit the joint for him, and he inhaled, thinking of the name *Lancelot Drugs*. There was something refreshing about the way it called itself *Lancelot Drugs* and not *Industries* or *Pharmaceuticals*. They were developing a new sleep aid, but testers reported fitful dreams. John worried briefly about Miller's cool appraisal of his empty seat. Yet almost immediately his anxiety dissolved. He thought of Ines and Art and that blue glass ashtray they used. Ines was such an unlikely pothead. He was always slightly put off when Veronica smoked—she became remote and usually went straight to sleep—but at this moment he could not imagine an offering more comforting, more essentially good, than this one.

He passed the joint back to Derek and hugged and kissed his daughter. He saw himself momentarily, saw what he was doing, but Clara was clean and well again. They sat for a few minutes while the baby played with her toes, bringing them all the way up to her mouth.

Without warning, she lurched forward in his arms. He turned her around and saw that her cheeks were flushed dark red. Then came the milk, like a geyser, shooting out of her mouth onto his chest. *Fool*, he cursed himself, muttering as he tried to wipe off the mess with his bare hand. *Fucking idiot*. It had taken only about forty minutes for her to get sick from the cow milk. He opened the car door and she kept going, vomiting onto the sand. The two small bath towels he'd brought from their room were soaked.

"She doesn't feel well," Derek observed.

"No, she doesn't," John said, kissing Clara's head.

"Hi, little girl," Derek said. He handed John his own towel, a thin but clean one covered in black and yellow stripes. John wrapped her in it and she looked like a bumblebee. The heaving finally stopped; she lay exhausted in his arms. Derek looked worried. "Is her mom here? Breast milk, they say, cures all."

"Ah, the tyranny of breast milk! Her mother isn't here," John said. This sounded rather grave and final, so he added, "She couldn't come." Derek furrowed his brow. "Listen, can you drive me to the store you mentioned? For goat milk."

On the way there, Clara's body felt loose and light, depleted.

John was shaken by her illness. Paranoia saturated him in waves. What had he done? He couldn't be high while she was sick. Fleetingly, a dreamy hope prevailed; clusters of goats brayed at the car, as they had on his way to Lord Harrington's Castle, encouraging in their abundance. There were so many goats, there had to be goat milk *somewhere*! Just as quickly, the snug, suffocating fear resumed.

"Who was Lord Harrington, anyway?" he asked, to break the silence.

"He was some English guy with a lot of money, a hemophiliac with a very pale wife and a daughter who drowned."

A daughter who drowned. John was stricken by the very phrase. A warm breeze came in and soothed his face. His high canted into little crests of pleasure, and for a moment the hemophilia just heightened Lord Harrington's glamour. The trees bent in almost complete arches, and the earth rose and fell in gentle hills. Giant white clouds spread above him. They passed through a small village with rows of pottery stands. Bowls, bowls, one after another, like all those bowls—some lovely and some useless—that they'd received as wedding gifts. Clara cleaved to his chest. "Why can't you sell your pottery here?" John asked, pointing to the roadside stands. He enjoyed the fact that the baby was letting him cuddle her. Usually she was too busy twisting away, investigating the world.

"I can, but I wouldn't make anything, or not enough. I make more in other ways, different jobs. I'm extremely poor, but I don't feel like I am," he said matter-of-factly.

On the way to the store, John imagined some exotic genius herbalist, an old, bearded black man selling "remedies." The

store would be all smoky, and there'd be anise and all Veronica's weird herbs and the essential goat milk. Instead, they
pulled up to a cinder-block shack decked out with Coca-Cola
signs and filled with as much primary-colored plastic as possible. Cases of beer lined one wall, and above them were post-
ers of bikini-clad Bajan beauties reclining on the rocks. Another
wall displayed beach buckets, umbrellas, and lotion, and a
third had a low-humming freezer that opened from the top to
reveal Tombstone frozen pizza. A glass-doored fridge was
filled with orange soda, Coke, and some mangy celery. The
aisles held canned things like peas, corn, and yams in olive-
green packaging that looked like it had been shipped from
England in the fifties.

Out of the corner of his eye, he saw a tall, dark-haired
woman examining a pair of blue plastic flip-flops. She had the
same purse as Veronica, an ungainly vanilla leather satchel
with a massive brass buckle, and was clearly disappointed with
the store. The purse, he knew, cost eleven hundred dollars.
He knew because he had bought it for his wife, at Ines's suggestion. What could be dumber? What could be grosser than
a purse that expensive? He had fallen into another life, another
world. He averted his eyes as she approached him. "Do you
have any idea where to get any decent diapers around here?"
she said with a conspiratorial hush, and gestured to a package
of Cheekies, the local diaper brand.

"Those are diapers," John said, grabbing a package off the
shelf; soon they'd run out. He stepped away, wanting to ally
himself with Derek.

"You can't get anything around here," she murmured to
no one in particular, and wandered off. John had been disap-

pointed in the store too, but now it seemed perfectly ade-
quate. He was high, and time was slipping away from him.

"Derek, I'm looking for goat milk. Do you see any? Do
you know if they have any? That's what bumblebee here
drinks."

"The dairy section," Derek said, making air quotes for
some reason as he pointed toward the back of the store. John
peered into a jumbled fridge, but the faces of cows were printed
on all the cartons. Cows everywhere, on each container he
picked up. Cows with huge black nostrils and misleading sweet
eyes. It was scary. A cow conspiracy was poisoning his daughter. "I don't think anyone really drinks goat," Derek ventured.

"No, only *insane*, affluent, overeducated American women,"
John said.

Derek brightened. "I know: Laura will have some."

"Who's Laura?" John asked. He was holding a container of
formula, thinking this would make it easy. Veronica wouldn't
know. But—he hadn't imagined this would happen—Veronica's
judgment had become intrinsic to his own.

"She's my fiancée's mother. She's everything you
described—except she's not American, she's Bajan. A crazy
old white lady, but she'll have it or at least know how to get
it." John bought some formula, just in case, and the package
of Cheekies and followed Derek to the car to go find Laura.

He felt fine again, cozy and cared for in the bucket seat as
he looked beyond the parking area and down into a valley
that was much greener and dewier than Lord Harrington's
side of the island. It was raining lightly, as the driver from the
airport had warned, and John squinted through the mist,
straining to see what Derek said was a rainbow.

"Oh, right, I see it," John said, even though he didn't.

As they sat there, Derek opened the glove compartment and showed John two different kinds of pot and explained the prices for each. Clara, damp on his chest, slept during the transaction. Evan was obliterated. And Veronica—well, she certainly would have understood this moment. Feeling suddenly compassionate, he wanted to tell her he could understand, he, *too*, could understand moments like this. He would call and tell her everything and she would *get* it. And she would *get* him. Clara gurgled and blew spit bubbles. She felt better. John stuffed the small plastic bag into his knapsack, full of hope.

As Derek drove over the hill approaching the west side, the landscape grew even softer and greener. John saw the golf course at the Glittering Sands, where Veronica's father, David Edelson, had once crushed him. John had scored a hundred and six in a round. No, he had not wanted to try golf; he'd rather have lolled on the beach with Veronica, propped up on their sides as they read novels and paused to read each other passages or to kiss. His girlfriend had become his wife and then a mother. It was amazing to realize that this was all Veronica. She permeated his whole adult history. The thought shook him, for there was essentially no adult version of John Reed—they'd met through Art when John was just twenty-five—without her. Here, he was stunningly singular, and it was both strange and elating. "Have you ever eaten here?" John asked Derek casually. He gestured toward a sign for the club, gilded letters on a white painted seashell.

"At the Glittering Sands? No way. Private club."

"My wife's family used to come here—I was here once. With them. They've got a great lunch buffet, and I'm sure they have goat milk—they have everything—or can get it. Should we stop and eat?"

"Man, this is the citadel, the fortress. You can't just go in and eat."

"You don't understand. They were members. We were. I've been here before. They have the best piña coladas in the world."

"You have, like, a card or something?"

"A card?"

"A membership card, to enter."

"It's not like that. I know the guys who work here; it'll be fine." John directed Derek through the first set of gates, flanked by huge bushes of pink bougainvillea. He wanted that club sandwich they had, a British type with an egg in it and too much mayonnaise; he wanted to take Clara to the kidney-shaped pool with the fountain in the middle. Driving through the gates was comforting to him, as if he had not gone away but had come back.

The world was getting smaller and smaller as wars teemed and connections stretched. These days, Arthur's favorite word was *globalization*. New York to the Caribbean was one cloth, when there was all of the Middle East to consider, the war in Iraq, natural disasters in Asia. In many ways, he and Clara hadn't really gone that far.

Derek drove slowly. Armed guards stared at the beat-up Corolla as it approached the next set of gates. The flowery scent, the essential hope that emanated from Derek, Clara's babbling—all this propelled him. "Man," Derek said, nearly stopping, "I think we should turn around."

"Don't be crazy, it's fine; the concierge can get me the goat

milk in, like, a minute, and you and I will have a nice lunch."
John remembered David Edelson with his six faxed newspapers
every morning, how the concierge had delivered them to him
on a silver tray while he sat at the beach. John's tiny column had
been in that pile, in the *Journal*, and he had sat with his future
father-in-law with a mixture of anticipation and fear as the
older man sifted through the stack and eventually found it. It
was embarrassing and wonderful. His own father never would
have done this: As Veronica and her mother busied themselves
with their hyper-conscientious applications of sunscreen in the
shade a distance away, Veronica's father, known as "the Edelson
Oracle," read aloud the words John had written.

"Rich families are odd," John had told Veronica later that
night when they were alone. "You can do *anything*—make clay
pendants of your genitalia, go to clowning school—and,
because the stakes are so slight, anything you do could be a
source of celebration."

"That's completely untrue. It's the opposite. I have to work
to get their approval," she'd said. She gestured to her bedside
table, piled high with books—*The German Expressionist Influ-
ence*, *The Dream of Chagall*, and a fat notebook with a mess of
papers tucked into it that would become her thesis.

He'd reached for her nude waist and embraced her. "You're
doing great," he said, understanding she needed to hear it. It
was less than a year into the relationship, and he could find no
flaw in her. He kissed her velvety ribs, her small hip bones.

"I have to do *more*. I have to prove myself. Don't you see
that?" Laughingly, she boxed him on the head. And she had
done great. She had published a chapter of her thesis in a prestigious journal and been offered a teaching job.

Later, he thought it had all been for pleasure, an entire degree *because she wanted to*, because she'd abandoned the field and moved on to public health. She said he was judgmental about this, but she'd misunderstood; he was envious of her ability to wander, to seek a career that satisfied her.

Someone was approaching the car. The guard's beige uniform was there, stretched tight around his crotch, framed by the car window. Derek opened his wallet to reveal his driver's license. "You have business here today?" John heard the voice ask.

Derek said, "My friend here is a member; I'm his driver." John bent down and waved at the guard. Then he revealed Clara's sleeping face from under the towel. She was warm but peaceful. The driver waved them forward a bit hesitantly. John could see him writing something down in a little pad as they drove away.

"You're my driver?" John asked.

"Well, I *am* driving you. It's no big deal." Derek shrugged.

"I don't want you to think you have to drive me around—"

"I don't. It's all right," he laughed. "I was going to this side of the island to see my fiancée, Monika, man. Remember? Don't get all troubled on me. We're okay."

"It's all good," John said, reassured. Derek was not his chauffeur, but John could not have gotten here so quickly without him. "Thanks for all this."

"Your girl seems better too."

"She does, I know." At that moment Clara woke up, stretching her head out of the carrier like a turtle, then retracting it when a shaft of bright sun hit her eyes. John kissed the cushiony spring of soft cheek. The next checkpoint was a small house where two men sat. One emerged and stood on the passenger side of the car, holding his holster and baton, for a slow minute.

He bent down eventually and addressed Derek. "Can I help you?"

"We're here for lunch," John said breezily.

The guard stood up and conferred for a while with his partner. He chuckled and took his time before he finally came back.

"Are you staying at the hotel?" he asked.

"I have before, and I'm back in town, so—"

"Are you checking in today?"

"No, I—"

"What's the name of the reservation?"

"Edelson. It was—"

The man turned away again and went into the little house. John saw him move very slowly, adjusting the buckle of his belt, laughing with the other man, and then, gradually, picking up the phone.

"You booked a room?" Derek asked, unsure.

"No, but these formalities—I mean, they're just enjoying the minuscule amount of power that they have."

The other man, younger and skinnier, approached this time. "There's no record of your reservation, sir. Is it perhaps under another name?" John could see the older man behind him, leaning back in his chair and lighting a thin brown cigarette.

"Can you ask him to come back?"

The young man looked worried and shook his head no.

"Look, there's no other name, but is this necessary? We only want to get some milk for my daughter here and have some lunch. I've stayed here before."

"We can't let anyone in without a booking, sir," he said. Beads of sweat broke out across his upper lip, which he'd probably just begun to shave.

John laughed. They didn't understand that he was coming *back*. Clara giggled too, as if he was playing with her. "Can I speak with your supervisor, then?"

"That's him," the boy said hopelessly, nodding toward the smoking guard.

"Well, then, *his* supervisor, the manager, or someone?"

When the boy left to speak with his supervisor, Derek said, "We can get the goat milk elsewhere, man. I'll get it for you. Don't worry."

"You don't have to do things for me. It's fine. Wait."

The young man returned with a cordless phone that looked ancient, the same oversize Panasonic from Veronica's apartment in the early nineties. Clara lunged at it and held on while John spoke. It was a woman this time—disaffected, distant, and cool, as if they'd brought the same one from Lord Harrington's Castle to disappoint him again.

"If you have an appointment, a booking of some sort, you may enter," she said. "Otherwise, you may not enter the premises."

"Fine, can you connect me with the restaurant, then? I'll book a reservation."

Derek was laughing and shaking his head.

"What?" John said to Derek as he was put on hold.

"Amazing," he said, smiling. "Americans. Actually, mainly New Yorkers."

"Trust me, Derek."

"Oh, I know you'll get what you want."

Derek turned off the ignition, melting the car and the three passengers into the road as John spoke to the hostess at the restaurant, the golf pro (as if he'd take a lesson), and then, finally, the spa, which were all booked solid. Sleepy voices told him, one following the other, that it was not possible, that he had to call quite far in advance, that the hotel was very busy at this time of year. Desconsolately, he gave up the Panasonic.

A cool betrayal rippled up through John's belly and settled in his throat; he felt the way he had in tenth grade when his girlfriend, Maria Chimay, a not very pretty freshman, had dumped him unexpectedly for an upperclassman. That night he'd gone to lock his bedroom door to masturbate—with or without Maria's rubbery hand jobs, he could still do this—and the lock, something from the hardware store he'd installed himself, crumbled off into his palm. Taking his chances, he'd done it anyway. He'd tried to summon Maria's mediocre face, her smooth shoulders, as he worked, but she'd vanished.

"What the fuck?" John said. "You'd think this was Nolita." Hadn't the name Edelson meant anything to them? They'd failed to understand the tinyness of the world.

Derek shrugged his shoulders. "They're just doing their jobs," he said, and smiled modestly while John glowered. Slowly, Derek turned on the ignition. Gingerly, he turned the car around, and they drove at a child's pace over the broken-seashell drive, past the abundant bushes of bougainvillea in their unreal hues, moving back past the damp green mounds of the golf course to the world outside the gates.

PART TWO

MEMORY

6

Saturday

Veronica

Veronica woke up happy. It was not the very common five-fifteen in the morning or even the marginally better five-forty but an otherwordly nine. She had slept for ten straight hours. Was her contentment purely chemical? She wanted to believe that her mind and not her body was in control, but after two full nights of sleep she felt purified, oiled like a machine that was finally, once again, in tune. She stretched as each limb came to life, to the future that was Irvington.

She'd have to tell Dr. Weiss, her former therapist, that hers was not a problem of the mind at all but one of the body. The body trumped the mind, and if you attended to it, with a special homemade formula, with sleep, a bedside tray of pills, all could be healed. On that awkward first visit back to therapy, after the baby was born, Veronica had wrapped Clara like a papoose and showed her to the older woman as evidence of her own worth: *Look what I made.*

She'd confessed to Dr. Weiss how she'd wanted her own mother; she'd wanted her to appear regularly, offering home-made lasagnas and remedies for clogged milk ducts, though this would have been entirely out of character. Veronica had lifted the bundle of the baby up to her cheek and kissed her. She didn't know how to explain to Dr. Weiss that she'd never been so happy and so miserable at the same time. But going to the Upper East Side with the diaper bag, the heavy car seat, and the baby was a feat she could manage only twice before she gave up.

There was a train leaving in one hour. A free hour was something fat and full, in which she'd read the entire *Times* and go out to eat duck farm eggs at her favorite place on 12th Street: one person, her knees neat under the counter. She would, in that fat gift of an hour, steep herself in the sensation, however temporary, of being rested. In the shower, she knew time was not something to be taken for granted. She could taste it, and it felt like soaring, like greatness.

She opened the shower door with a vague disappointment: John was not there to hear about what she'd do with an hour. How could she have been angry at him yesterday? He had given her the hour! In fact, he'd given her twenty-four.

If she left even later, she'd have time to draft the entire proposal for the Jasper School lunches with inspiration (for she *did* want to overhaul what students at Jasper ate). This was her *contribution*, work that mattered, not the aesthetic reverie she'd inherited from her mother. Although lately she wondered where that reverie had gone; her love of paintings had abandoned her. She missed seeing with insight. As she fastened her bra, a pigeon worked at tapping a pane of glass. He paused and fixed a red eye on hers. "What?" she said. She stared back at the bird, searching for some nuanced gradation in his urban feathers, but there was none. They were gray. She returned to the desk and enlarged the train schedule to fill the computer screen. She could pick her hour. If she left for Irvington even later, she might go to MoMA before she made it to Grand Central. She opened her phone to call Irvington, but before she had a chance, it rang.

It was Art, and he was whispering. "Can we meet at Greek Statuary?" Before Clara was born, Veronica had wandered the Greek galleries at the Metropolitan Museum almost every weekend.

"Why are you whispering?"

His voice returned to normal volume. "Ines just got in the shower; I can talk. You know how I never got her a diamond engagement ring—remember how I was against it? All the evil mining practices?"

"Uh-huh."

"Well, now, since we're having a baby—even though I think this is the foulest example of late-stage capitalism—there's this thing, a push ring, and I want to get one for her. I need your help."

She couldn't help laughing. *"A push ring?"*

"I didn't coin the phrase."

"You've found no correlation between possessions and happiness, remember?"

"On some level they correlate, if there's a measurable

difference—like having a house versus being homeless; it's complicated. Money doesn't make people happier, though. We know that. Except for an increase that lifts one out of poverty. But Ines is so down; come help me look this morning while she's at prenatal yoga."

"You have months to pick a ring. What about your *moral code*?" Art loved to say *moral code*. It was one of his favorite phrases, along with *blighted* when discussing an abandoned neighborhood and *mature trees* when discussing a very established one.

"It's a slackening, frankly. On my part. But I want to do it now, not in six months."

Ines *had* been through hell, and she would love diamonds and wouldn't care where in the world they came from. "I guess I could take the later train." It was a bright day, and the unfiltered winter light spilled on the bare floor. Shopping on a Saturday seemed sort of touristy and nice. Art suggested they meet at the very obvious Tiffany's.

"You have no idea how hard I'm going to hug you when I see you," he said.

"I think I have an idea." The plan cheered her up. Forget pushing: He could give Ines the ring right away to celebrate the pregnancy. She dialed Irvington.

"You've reached Evan and Muriel Reed," a recording began. Muriel's voice, recorded before Evan's death, wavered slightly as if with prescience. But then it continued with the bold assurance, the confidence, of the most deeply enmeshed couples, who assumed they'd never part. Muriel overenunciated each numeral, mistrustful of this simple technology. But there was a lilt in her voice that was emblematic of the Reeds—the

forever-empathic Reeds—who made you feel both cared for and slightly smaller, with their wise, seasoned assurances. Veronica heard Muriel's fallibility too; she'd not yet changed the recording to delete Evan, and this moved Veronica so sharply that tears sprang to her eyes.

"Muriel, hi," she said. "Can you guys pick up?" They must have gone out for bagels. "It's Veronica. Can you tell John I'm on the one o'clock train that arrives at one forty-six, so he can get me at the station? Kiss Clara for me. I'll see you soon. Bye." She called John's cell, and the recording said that the customer was *"out of range."* That was bizarre. Their service was always screwing up.

She tossed the useless phone on the bed. Why had he not called this morning? She sulked on the radiator by the window. As she stood up, one of John's cactuses, a dry, under-nourished husk, scratched her bare thigh. It was a *cactus* and he forgot to water it enough. She squeezed the cut until it bled. She'd always disliked the plants, and now she had reason to hate them; she opened the window and threw it out. The clay pot made a satisfying crash in the alleyway.

In the cab uptown, Veronica was suspiciously happy again. It was necessary, she told herself, to give in to friendship, despite what her morning's original goals had been. Alone, a veil was lifting, the texture of the world returning to her. She found a red cotton hat of Clara's in her purse and held it to her face. Her daughter was made of pure sugar.

The cab lolled to a stop at a red light near Union Square. Feathers and a lone plastic bag whirled up into the shaft between two buildings. On the corner she saw the familiar Happy Deli, with its crisp yellow awning.

"The formula!" she said; there was no way that John had brought enough. She leaned forward to speak to the driver. "You can stop here." The car glided to the corner. The Turkish deli owners knew her and smiled as she walked back to the dairy section and selected two containers of organic goat milk. She paid and took a few swigs of the goat milk to make room for the herbs, then emptied one packet—it made her feel safe to always have them on hand—into the container. She shook the bottle, then checked to make sure it was well blended.

John and Muriel were probably rushing around the gourmet market in Dobbs Ferry by now, looking for more goat milk while Clara grew hungrier. He could call to reassure her. He was taking her for granted, forgetting about her. Maybe she took him for granted. Art's romantic mission was inspiring. She and John hadn't surprised each other in a long time.

She walked past the prenatal yoga studio where Ines was strengthening her pelvic floor. It was the same studio where John and Veronica had endured the birthing class. The teacher, an unwavering yet timid woman named Naomi (Art said *of course* her name was Naomi), had extolled the virtues of natural childbirth and passed around totemic items that one could take into the birthing room, like the pilly hand-knit red stirrup warmers she herself had used, or a scented candle, or "a favorite CD," Naomi had said in a high-pitched voice, displaying one by Kate Bush.

One evening she had passed around a bowl of ice, urging each woman and her partner to hold a cube in the palm of their hand while practicing breathing through the discomfort. Veronica's palm burned slightly, then grew a little numb. The ice melted fast, dripping onto the wooden floor. Naomi scurried around the circle, drying the floor with a gray cloth. Veronica could cup ice for days.

John had raised his hand. "You said discomfort. Do you mean of *childbirth*?" Naomi nodded. "It must be harder than holding a piece of ice in your hand." The women in the room murmured their assent. Veronica had loved him for saying something.

Despite the incident with the ice, Naomi's own birth story was inspiring. Naomi had labored for six hours with no interventions and no complications. The photos of her own pink-cheeked toddlers seemed like evidence of her success. Naomi had made specific instructions in her birth plan; she would avoid all drugs and monitoring and would labor in a tub of warm water. She had not said explicitly that her good planning had caused her happy outcome, but that was the very powerful suggestion. Veronica had maintained this ideal in her mind for months. She hoped that the birthing class would quell her fears, but as the weeks passed her terror mounted.

She kept searching for some shred of comfort, some connection to the other women present—they were going through it together, all larger each week than they had been the one before—but the vague repetitive inquiry "Where are you delivering?" never led to much beyond the name of the hospital or birthing center.

As much as she wanted to be natural, she wanted to be safe. Veronica's OBGYNs, who Art said represented the "medical industrial complex," stressed safety. They relied on testing and statistics and informed decisions. They were, admittedly,

modern. They would preempt all disaster with their information. They quoted percentages and rates of success. They
harped on your fear. At the same time they would entertain
no possibility of failure. It was impossible to fully trust the fic-
tions of her doctors or Naomi.

In the end, Dr. Berlin had stuck to protocols, forcing the
testing and then the labor, when there was no sign of labor
at all, because Veronica was thirty-five and had been pregnant
for forty weeks. Thirty hours of Pitocin had made the uterus
paper-thin. The massive bleeding of the uterus could not be
stopped and led to the hysterectomy. The refrain of the birthing class, about the domino effect, about one thing leading to
another, had been true.

John, after his initial resistance (he'd said there were about
ten thousand things he'd rather do on a Sunday afternoon
than attend the birthing class) and their laughter about the ice
cubes, had never complained again. She saw now how he had
supported her. He had let her believe what she attested to.

A green diamond glittered on Art's pinkie. "The ring makes
you look like a gangster," Veronica said.

"Too much?" he asked, waggling his fingers.

"A colored stone can be very chic," said a blond saleswoman
with total sincerity, a bracelet of keys jingling on her wrist.
Veronica nodded politely, then peered into the cabinet while Art
consulted his phone, scrolling through his e-mail.

"I think Ines likes simpler things—maybe this eternity band,"
Veronica said, slipping into the saleswoman's vocabulary. She
pointed at a small platinum band ringed with tiny diamonds.

The woman nodded with approval and placed it on a blue velvet tray. "Holy shit," Art said, staring at the phone in his palm.

"What?" Veronica asked.

"Nothing. A work thing."

Art slipped various rings onto Veronica's fingers, shoving them too roughly over her knuckles.

"Ouch!" she said.

"Sorry."

"How are *you* doing," she asked, "about the funny test result?"

"I'm optimistic. I'm sure it's an error," he said, but he looked worried.

"That's what John would probably say."

"Have you *heard* from John today?" he asked, relinquishing an entire tray back to the saleswoman.

"He gets very wrapped up with Muriel, talking about Evan and going through stuff in the garage. We're playing phone tag." Art wandered away to a different counter. "Do you see anything you like?" she asked, catching up with him.

He wiped some imaginary drip from his nose with his thumb and moved to yet another counter, so she found herself following him.

"Why are you moving so fast? You're not even looking."

"Okay, let's focus," he said.

"You look like you're holding your breath or something."

"Maybe we should take some pictures of these." Art crouched down to look into a glass cabinet of emerald rings. Veronica checked her watch while Art started to snap photos. Hopefully Clara had had enough of the special formula to get her to this moment, which was eleven-forty. A voice asked her if anything *grabbed her fancy.*

"They're all lovely," she said, growing impatient with Art.

He popped up and walked away again. They stared down at rings made to look like they were from antiquity. Amulets, Roman twists, and braids of gold. Veronica said, "Remember, today you're just seeing what's out there. You're not buying anything. She'll love whatever you get."

"No she won't. Ines?"

Veronica sighed. "Well, what are you gravitating toward, Art? What do *you* like?"

"I have to borrow money from the furrier for this ring. I want her to love it." Art called his father, Larry Greene, "the furrier," because he was one.

"You have time," she said. Once again, she did not; she had no time. The expansive moment in the shower was an illusion. She was walking around in the vessel that was her body, carrying her various parts—the necessary liver and the unnecessary appendix. Even if she left now, she was probably going to miss the twelve o'clock train.

Art waved his hand like an old pro. "By the time I get the image over to Abe in the diamond district and he copies it— you never want to buy retail, Veronica."

"Aren't you the expert all of a sudden. Who's Abe?"

"Abe Zelnick—he's an old friend of my dad. A jeweler. I'm going today. He's on Forty-seventh. Can you come?"

"I'm helping you now. I'm trying to catch a train. I don't have time." Her scar seemed to tighten and then release.

"John will be fine without you," Art said, as he studied a large diamond he could never afford. "The four C's," he murmured. "Color, cut, carat, and—*hell*, what was the last one?"

"John will be fine without me?" The carpeted ground

shifted beneath her. Where was John? Art's eyes dodged around the glass case. They had to be back from Dobbs Ferry by now.

"I meant, taking care of the baby. But you know what, pumpkin—"

"I'm not your pumpkin, Art."

People around them hushed and stepped away, clearing a berth for their argument.

"Jeez, John was right, you know that?"

"He was right?"

"Forget it."

"You know, I don't even want to hear it," she said, striding ahead of him.

"Wait!"

She faced him. "Why should I wait? I have very little time. Do you understand that? You couldn't possibly. I'm doing you a favor. This is the first Saturday—" She stopped herself. He stared up at her—he was *that* short—his stocky arms folded across his chest. His slightly imperious smile made her continue. "You two get together and gripe about your wives, about all your deprivations. You poor, poor things. It's unbelievable! I don't know what he told you, but it's none of your business, Art!" She trembled slightly, her heart racing.

"You have gone completely . . ." He paused and then murmured, "Bitch," under his breath.

"*Gone bitch*? Who says that? Since when is *gone bitch* an expression?"

"Excuse me, you've changed, okay? *You have changed.*"

She looked up at the ceiling, where small halogen lights were embedded in the coffered wood. Little rainbow prisms danced about the rafters; there was still beauty. She could find it. She could see it again. But stones kept filling her throat, little pebbles, like something raw and undigested. She felt Art's thick hand on her elbow and flicked it off.

"What do you expect? I had a child." The blond saleswoman with the bracelet of keys walked by and lowered her eyes. "But it's good, the change. You know what Clara does?" Veronica improvised. "She makes everything perfectly clear; she breeds conviction and shows me what's true. The false stands out in high relief. Like you right now."

A box of tissues appeared on the counter near her elbow, and she took one, out of habit. Absently, she separated the two layers. After, she got angry this new way. These flashes of total conviction almost felt good. It was true: Clara set the priorities. There was *nothing* that meant more than her.

As Veronica walked toward the elevator, Art scuttled behind her, trying to catch up. It looked like a lover's quarrel. They were having the fight that she and John had avoided for the past six months.

A group of Japanese tourists stood and watched the elevator dial move. A woman in a pink sweater set peered through a handheld camera and recorded the moving dial. They were happy tourists, enamored of everything. In your own city you were stuck with yourself. And John? John's life, swirling and changeable—his life was going on in Irvington without her.

That was all. Was it so bad? Was this the stony dam that a marriage got to, the place where it faltered, at a simple juncture like a trip to your mother's during which you just *don't* miss your wife?

John and Muriel might be hunched over photos of Evan in the Peace Corps as Clara slept. Evan, the great liberal. John was swept up by him all over again. Art stood silently beside her. The elevator was taking forever.

"V, sorry, okay?" Art said. "I didn't mean anything about John." He was panting a little and completely sweaty. "I really need your help this afternoon."

"I've already helped you," she said, trying to be remain icy, but the familiar, cold cloak of *after* was parting, lifting at the seams. "I came here, I pointed you toward the more-subtle rings that I thought Ines would like." She picked up her phone and looked at it. It was noon, and, unbelievably, there was no call from John. The word HI flitted across her screen, from Damon. She smiled but deleted the greeting and looked up; the woman in pink was now filming another tourist who was filming that elevator dial. She and Art exchanged a brief look and then a smile. Art began to laugh and then quake silently, which made Veronica laugh. He erupted audibly, and then she did too. They were still recovering as they entered the silent elevator. She would try to call John on the street.

She wanted John's voice, *his* solicitousness. Her renewed desire for her husband was like the tip of something delicious that she couldn't get enough of, the pointed bottom of an ice cream cone. But she considered John's eerily complete silence. She wouldn't go just yet. She needed to stop thinking. She turned to Art. "Do you want to get some lunch? Before I get the train, I mean?" She wouldn't go just yet. She pictured the condensation on a glass of cold white wine. Neither Ines nor John ever drank during the day. It made Ines too sleepy, she said. John claimed he had a surplus of intense feelings and didn't need to have any more. He was happy enough, he said, and didn't need to become happier. But Veronica always needed to be happier, and Art always said yes.

7

Saturday

John

"What kind of name is *Glittering Sands*, anyway?" John asked Derek as they drove away.

"Hey, it's your club, man."

"Clearly it is *not* my club. I mean, *Glittering Sands*? They might as well call it dreamland, fucking dreamland." Derek's silent rejoinder was a resounding affirmation. It was dreamland. It was totally unreal; the hotel was a white plastic cutout, a turreted fluffy wedding cake pasted onto the turquoise sea. Clara was a writhing mass on his chest, her very existence mind-blowing. Veronica was a specter, a thing called a wife. He had failed to get back in touch with the office. Even his job was beginning to feel imaginary. All of it, his whole life, was vanishing.

He was falling into this vortex; what had he done? He pictured yesterday's meeting. John could see Lloyd Miller flipping through John's scant report on Lancelot Drugs, fuming; a company Miller had discovered, a very attractive potential investment, postponed by a lazy and absentee stringer.

As they pulled into the drive at Laura Simpson's antiques shop, there was solidity again. He identified Derek's girlfriend, Monika, right away; she was the blond, pregnant one, playing with a rough little dog the color of a Triscuit on the crab grass. There were several women in front of the shop, but John knew instinctively which was the girlfriend. Her legs were muscular, and there was something blanched and stripped about her face—too much sun at one point in her life and spotty dental work. They were having some kind of tea or shower for Monika, and the other women—both white and black—drifted away, saying goodbye. Monika smiled when she found Derek, and they embraced while her gargantuan belly pointed to one side. John watched them kiss, then turned away when she caught his eye.

"Hey, don't hit Daddy," she said in a Bajan accent, because Clara had started a game, swatting at John's face as they walked from the car. "She's adorable, hi," Monika said, extending her hand to shake his.

John's voice cracked as he introduced himself. For years with Veronica, he hadn't really noticed other women; lately he'd begun to again—a strand of golden hair that grazed a jawline, fine-boned ankles—though he was guilty only of looking. When they'd returned from the hospital, his wife's strangeness terrified him. She'd remained huge but was deflated, fine gray hairs had begun to colonize her temples, and a layer of dank white flesh shone over the top of her maternity jeans. She was bloated and fogged and AMA, as they'd said in the hospital—

of advanced maternal age. She was a piece of a demographic, and he was too. To think, they'd once imagined they were unique! They were ordinary, wholly defined by their circumstances.

Looking at Monika, he was outside any category. Monika's pink complexion and open expression were so unsuspecting of her own future.

Something flickered in Derek's gaze as he noticed John, a shell of pain or recognition, and he let go of Monika's hand. "John needs goat milk, and I had a feeling you or your mum would know where to get some," he told her.

"Sure. There's this little health-food store in Bridgetown that probably has it." She looked down. With the toe of her sandal, she nudged some pebbles around the base of a red-flowering tree.

"There are these herbs that go with it," John said to no one in particular, as Laura—*Mum*—emerged. A large, freckled woman, she burst out of a lush but messy garden set up in a corner of the yard, which abutted a wide, flat field. She had Monika's pink skin tone and overbleached hair. She wore an enormous, slightly transparent blue muumuu, which ruffled in the breeze. Brambles stuck to the muumuu and crackled behind her as she moved forward. They were wonderful, Monika and Laura. "She hit she dad?" Laura said, as she approached and casually took the baby away from John. Clara grew anxious and twisted toward her father and was handed back to him. Ordinarily, Clara's default holder was Veronica. Things had been easy for John. He pictured Veronica here, perching on the arm of a mahogany overseer's chair in the shade while she sipped a piña colada. For the first time since he'd landed, he was aware of missing her. "She wants a look in the shop," Laura said, as she led them into her store. Several mangy dogs lay in their path, on the cool concrete steps and trampled gardenias. "Her mum is here too?" Laura asked.

"She's actually not here," he said, jostling the baby.

"Sorry to hear it," Laura said in a mournful tone, as if Veronica had died. She draped a fat arm around his shoulder very briefly as she ushered him inside. He didn't correct her. As he crossed the dusty threshold of the store, he didn't tell her that Veronica was alive. His own morbidity chilled him. As Derek explained to Laura that they were heading to the health-food store, John couldn't stop his eyes from roving again and again to Monika's belly.

Laura said, "Maybe you can bring something back for her."

"For who?" John said, adjusting Clara as she started to whimper and twist. Clara then arched her back stiffly, pulling away from him as if to catapult herself out of his arms. *You can hold 'em and not hold 'em, like a bar of soap!* Rosemary would have said before whisking her away. But now there was no one to help him, and nothing could soothe Clara.

"A present for her mum," Laura replied, easily speaking over Clara's crying. He was relieved; it was as if Laura had just told him that Veronica was not dead. Laura produced a cornflower-blue-and-white ceramic statuette of a cherubic toddler cuddling a dog with dopey eyes. "These are from Spain. They happen to be collector's items. They're fine bone china." John examined the object briefly, as if he were considering buying it. A calmness pervaded as he fondled the blue glazed ear of the dog: No one, except for perhaps Clara, thought Veronica was permanently gone.

"Look at the doggy, sweetie," John said. Clara stopped crying for a moment, intrigued by the figure. John looked over the baby and around the dusky antiques shop for a phone.

Derek was sitting nearby in a mahogany rocking chair with Monika—giggling and overblown—on his lap. That stomach! He'd never seen anything that ripe, that delicious. Without thinking, he squatted to touch it. Then Clara did too; she leaned her head onto Monika's belly. Monika laughed, but John could see Derek's face behind her, darkening again. Perhaps Derek was simply scowling at the score of a cricket game on the TV that was propped in the corner.

John turned to find Laura and the phone, but she'd wandered away. "Do you think I could use your phone?" he called out. "Mine isn't working." He found Laura dusting a tea set in the next room and stood watching the green feather duster dance in the white heat. He wanted to ask her again but she looked up at him blankly, as she would to any customer, any stranger in her shop. He was a stranger in her shop. "Yes?" Laura said, but John heard Monika playfully beeping the horn as she and Derek sat waiting in the car.

Clara cried for the entire twenty-minute drive to Bridgetown. There was traffic, and young men in synthetic pants wandered between the cars, jaywalking. John was sweltering but didn't dare loosen Clara from the carrier; it was all that protected her.

They found the stuff in the back of the health-food store, in dusty cardboard boxes. Clara drank a lot of goat milk and passed out on the way back to Laura's, leaving a deep-brown stain on John's belly where her diaper had leaked. His high was fading but Derek seemed friendly again, offering him a clean T-shirt from his car.

Laura had a tray of glasses and a pitcher of rum punch waiting when they arrived, and she signaled them to follow her. They cut through the brambly garden and into the polo field, where there were only the sounds of the wind and horses' hooves and the occasional whack on the ball. About thirty white people dressed in pastel colors were already seated, in rows, under a striped canopy. John was relieved not to have to speak. He took a few large sips of his cold drink. He'd been parched. The cinnamon and sugar were sticky on his lips. Then he crouched on the grass behind the audience and changed the soiled diaper. Clara grabbed the swizzle stick from his glass and licked it, her eyes happy again.

When the baby was clean, John knelt in the grass and drained his glass quickly; Laura appeared and handed him another one. Now that he'd fed Clara goat's milk, albeit without the special herbs, Veronica receded in his mind.

"Come sit," Laura said, ushering him to the front row, where she had saved four seats.

"Here?" John said, surprised.

"I married that one," she whispered, pointing to a man attached to a horse, trundling past in a puff of cologne, thunder dirt, and hay. Where Laura was flabby, her husband was taut; where she was loose, he was chiseled. He was a gorgeous man. An athlete married to this lovely unkempt woman. Their physical incongruity signaled a deep connection. They were the real thing. The thing that Muriel and Evan had been.

The baby was facing out and kicking her feet. The straps

of the Björn, now wet with perspiration, dug into his shoulders and back. It was shocking how much he wanted to put her down, to hand her to someone else, but the drink was perfectly spicy and cold, the sunlight was softening, dappling, under the shade of the tent. He would tell Veronica about it all soon. He could remember her. He could remember her finger tracing the edge of her beer glass the first time they met. How smooth and unlined her fingers were, like new pencils. He would tell her this. With this resolution, he started to rise to go find a phone.

Behind him, the sound of the mallet hitting the ball was both new and familiar: like a baseball thwack but cleaner, sharper. He had leaned down to get a zwieback toast from the diaper bag at his feet when the ball met his temple.

There was blood on his fingertips as he held them up above his face. Fingers that were pink sausages. A hammer beat in his metal skull. None of this was as frightening as the emptiness in his arms, the space where Clara had been. He sat up fast, despite his pounding head. He was on a cot inside a white tent, and a woman's tanned legs were beside him, like roots growing out of the ground. It was Monika, but Clara was gone.

"Are you all right?" she said.

He stood up and tore open the sash on the door, as if Clara might be sitting on the grass playing with a hibiscus. But she was not there. Farther afield, the game was continuing, but she was not over in the audience where he'd last held her, where Derek now sat disconsolately—this time he was sure of it—sipping his drink.

"She's had some bad diarrhea," Monika's voice said. "Mum is cleaning her off in the house. You both need to go see Dr. Tisbury in Speightstown."

Speightstown. It sounded like Spitestown. Not Bridgetown or some other town. Spite and retribution town. A long time ago he had climbed into a cab on Canal Street and driven away. This woman named Monika, who smelled of patchouli—how had he not recognized it before—was looking into his face, asking again if he was all right. Her eyes were blue and spacious; inadvertently, he inhaled her scent. His first real girlfriend at Amherst had worn the oil, and it always reminded him of sex. He didn't even like the smell of patchouli. Quite suddenly he did not like Monika—a stranger—at all. He craved the familiar, his wife. He ran toward the house, his head pounding, to find Clara. Monika shouted, "Slow down. You may have a concussion!" She said something else he couldn't make out, about heads and concussions and things that seemed wildly irrelevant. Panting, she caught up to him. "John, stop, you're hurt."

"I'm fine!" he muttered.

"You need to take it easy," Monika said, her voice a bit distant, wary.

A cool dread skittered across his chest. He needed to see Clara. He walked fast and couldn't answer Monika. Nothing mattered but the empty BabyBjörn and Laura saying. "Her mum is here too?" as innocently as if Veronica had never been in danger.

He was aware of Monika's belly as she hurried along beside him. It had reached a stage that was familiar to John, both round and pointed at the same time: a giant egg-arrow, with all the fragility and determination of such a thing. The enormous oval shook as she moved. Initially alluring, Monika's body now haunted him.

John rushed across the lawn holding his pulsing head. With each step he took, his head seized. He mounted the steps to Laura's shop two at a stride, accidentally squashing the ear of an old boxer, who wailed in pain.

8

Saturday

Veronica

Veronica listened as Arthur called Ines from the Oyster Bar to tell her what he was having for lunch. "No, the white one," he said, "with heavy cream," referring to his chowder. Lately, John didn't care what Veronica ate. Ines must've been interested, because Veronica heard Arthur say, "No, no, not dinner rolls, the little crackers—you know, in the packets. . . . Old drunk men at the bar, uh-huh, as usual. . . ." He laughed and winked at Veronica. "And some drunk women too."

Veronica smiled at him across the leather booth and licked cream off the back of her thumb. Yes, she was eating heavy cream. In a bar. The "food Nazi," as John had called her, who'd arrived after the birth, was gone. Her lips were thick from the two martinis, which had done their magic of simultaneously slowing down and speeding up time; they mitigated anything that competed with the pleasure they provided, so that missing her one P.M. train to see Clara, and then missing the two P.M., was tolerable. She had left messages about being remiss on both numbers. But *he* was the one who was remiss. *John.* She mouthed his name a few times, until the name became a sound and the sound became strange. When Art hung up, she asked, "How's Ines doing? Is she all right?"

"She's still upset but very limber. Apparently they did a lot of hip openers." Art grinned, delighted at the thought of his wife's hips.

"She's still pretty down?"

"Yup. It's abstract for me. For her . . . it's inside her. She puts—every time—the sonogram photo on the kitchen counter. They look like snails, but it's a real person—you tell yourself that—and then it's suddenly *not.*" He began chewing on his olives very fast.

"I'm sorry."

"This one has to not do that, you know?" He looked away for a long moment. "The damage is accruing for her. It just can't happen to her again."

"No, no, it can't happen. It won't."

"Can you distract her later, take her out to dinner? We could all go."

"You think John will be back any minute, right?" She stared at Art as he spread his short fingers out on the red-and-white-checked tablecloth and studied them. "Art?"

"Hell yes, before you can say Jack Robinson, pumpkin! Sorry, sorry, you're not my pumpkin. These are good. You want another?" He gestured with a cloudy martini glass, then plucked out the extra blue-cheese-stuffed olive at its base.

"I should probably eat more first," Veronica said, opening her package of saltines and shaking it into the bowl as Arthur moved to the bar. The crackers were crisp and blended well with the leftover chowder. She wanted to lick the bowl.

Art returned with two martinis, even though she'd said no, and placed one before her. "What you should probably do is come with me to the diamond district. I'm going for only a minute, before we meet Ines."

"I'm . . . I need to speak to John and find out what's going on."

"I think you should stay." Arthur looked at the edge of the Jasper School lunch-project folder emerging from her handbag. "What you should do is advocate a steady diet of heavy cream and vodka for all second-graders," he said, "and stay in the city with us."

"Shit." Veronica bit her lip. "I have to get that done by Tuesday," she said. Time was speeding up, sifting away, and she'd accomplished nothing.

"Weren't you going to be a curator once upon a time?"

"I don't have a doctorate, only my master's. And I'm not going to be a docent like my mother." She was a mother; she had responsibilities Art couldn't fathom, a fitted path, intractable and set.

"Ah, docents. I love a docent!"

She was sipping the new drink and laughing again. "No you don't. Trust me."

"Yes I do, their unbridled enthusiasm, I do."

Veronica's mother, Annalena, had woken up one morning when Veronica was five and decided her life was worthless.

She had sat up in bed in a tiny peach silk bed jacket—it was fey and oddly Victorian—crying. "It's time," she had said when Veronica had dared to ask what was wrong, "for me to continue my education."

Then every Tuesday morning Annalena began to drive away in her forest-green BMW to study Early American furniture at Winterthur, the du Pont mansion in Delaware. She wouldn't return all that day or anytime within the blank and dull expanse of the next, which Veronica was told was called Wednesday. And Annalena didn't come back most of the next interminable day, called Thursday. Veronica would insist on waiting up for her mother but would always fall asleep, still in her clothes, on the nanny's tiny twin bed in her little room off the kitchen. Art was repeating, "Unbridled, totally unbridled," as he played with his glass.

"I'd thought all these things—what I would be when I grew up—would be resolved by now, but it's all much more complicated with a child."

Annalena would sneak into the tiny room to greet her, her cheeks smelling like winter and her fur coat staticky. She'd hug Veronica more passionately than usual and talk about her program in American Material Culture, which she called "the study of people and their things," about colonial craftsmanship or spindles.

Art stuffed two more large olives in his cheeks and tried to chew them at one time. "I don't know how you've become this do-gooder type. It's a WASPy thing. You think it's your duty to *serve*."

"I like what I do." She didn't want to be like her mother, enamored with aesthetics at the expense of human relationships. She wanted to *contribute*, as Muriel and Evan had always contributed.

She looked at her phone. It was horrible. A loathsome metal rectangle she kept glued in her hand with devotion. There was nothing from John. Rage crept in, warming her in places like her cheeks and chest while her hands turned to ice. She was getting drunk.

Arthur leaned across the table. "Are you all right?"

"I don't know." She shook her head as tears slipped from her eyes, landing in fat drops on the gingham tablecloth.

"Why don't you go home and sleep this off? I'll get the check."

"I can't rest. I need to get up there. I haven't actually *spoken* with him."

"You should take a break. Stay here. Ines could use your company tonight."

"I should be rushing up there to see my baby."

"She's fine."

"Tell me I'm not a bad mother." John would not tell her that, she was sure. "See, Ines is far too honest and might start pointing out my shortcomings, but you—you're much better at flattery. Oh, and this is my last drink. Don't even try getting me into any trouble tonight."

Trouble had begun during a heat wave in late September, on a Friday afternoon when Clara was ten weeks old and Veronica's prescription for pain meds had just run out. The pharmacist told her, "Most patients stop taking this after a week or two," and Veronica had hung up, stung by the unnecessary comment. John found her standing in the center of the loft with the phone in her hand. He squeezed her shoulders. "You should go out—go to the movie," he said.

"You think?" Ines had invited her to see *The Motorcycle Diaries.*

"I do. It'd be good for you."

Rosemary, in her white squeaky shoes, lumbered by, carrying the sleeping baby to her crib in one arm. How did she get Clara to sleep like that, so solemn, almost formal, in her tight wrap?

Weeks had passed, but the loop of discourse played endlessly in her brain: She'd been cut and dismembered. Parts were taken out and put back in. Regardless of what had happened that night, she needed to feed her baby. A painful scab had formed on each breast. The infection had worsened, but she needed to keep Clara alive. She'd let the baby latch on for a minute or two, but it was excruciating. She was failing to do what was most elemental.

"You should go," John had said. He spoke to her from some great muffled distance. She couldn't get through that space and didn't have the energy to protest, although leaving the house now, leaving Clara while on her ostensible maternity leave, felt like capitulation.

She had mixed the meager one ounce of milk she'd been able to pump with the new goat formula and stored it in the refrigerator, then moved hesitantly into the elevator and onto the baking street. She was not free: She was incomplete without them. The cloud that surrounded her was amplified by the humidity. When Veronica arrived at the apartment, Art was sitting in the red chair like the Cheshire cat. "Art has an idea," Ines said, rolling her eyes but smiling too as she stood by the air conditioner in a lavender bra. The atmosphere was cool but stale, but it was clarifying to be someplace else. Art opened his palm, where three small white pills rested. "John wouldn't be interested, but the three of us might be," he said.

They looked wonderful, cutting through the haze, precise and finite as punctuation. How she wanted to gobble them up. "What are they?" she asked.

"X," Ines said with deliberate nonchalance.

"Wow." She'd never tried Ecstasy. The dot looked so clean, like a piece of candy. "No, thanks. But do you have any Vicodin?" There were rows and rows of pills in their medicine cabinet. There had to be some.

"Out of vikes," Art said. "This'll be better."

Veronica looked at her watch as if disinterested, then flipped through an issue of *Dwell* that lay on the coffee table. In a glossy spread, a couple with a towheaded toddler emerged from a wood-paneled RV. "I'd rather see the movie."

Art ignored her protest while Ines pointed out an Eames chair in the magazine that she especially liked. "I took some last week with some people from Bard. It's all good," Art said, "F-ones. It might make you a little queasy at first, but after that, no problem."

Ines quickly said, "No pressure."

"I can't, but you two go ahead," Veronica said. When she got home she would try pumping again. She had drunk three cups of fenugreek tea to improve lactation, and the cloying sweet taste still clung to her teeth. How much could she hope to get? Another half an ounce, at most. Clara needed at least four ounces in a feeding. Ines glanced at Arthur while slipping her T-shirt back on.

"You know, he has a really reliable source," she told Veronica. Her new vulnerability muddied her volition. She didn't know what she wanted. Maybe she only wanted to forget for the evening. It was safe if Art said so. But she couldn't.

Her hand dangled in her purse and clutched the empty prescription bottle. Her incision pulled as she adjusted the waist of her still-tight jeans. "I could use some Advil if you have it. Maybe a beer."

Ines went to the fridge, then handed her a Stella Artois.

Ines and Art proceeded as if she weren't there, swallowing the pills with a bottle of water. For a few minutes they had penetrated that fuzzy distance. Now she was alone again. She rose as if to go to the movie, but she was not up for it, being by herself in the dark, and she found herself sitting back down on the sofa. She would go home, take the baby from Rosemary, be a mother. But tears of exhaustion stung her eyes. There was no needle, no smoke, no totemic feature that made the drug seem transgressive. The little white dot sat before her on the glass table.

"I'm not really doing this," she said as she swallowed the dot.

They wandered into Central Park to see what they would see. People were everywhere, ambling along in the heat, barefoot, damp-skinned, loud on their cellphones, vibrant in their new dresses, their odors. It felt good to sweat. In the beginning she threw up in a bush next to Sheep Meadow and then felt a bit better. She kept sweating more and more and it was like being washed, some sort of wringing out that she needed. She didn't know how much time had passed before she felt uncommonly good. Her body was loose and relaxed, her skin like some miraculous silky tube she'd been poured into. She adored her friends, touching the smooth whiteness of Ines's teeth, threading her fingers through the black spiral curls of her hair. Art had brought a sprayer and gave each of their faces a mist. Veronica told stories about Clara, about how her wrists and ankles were becoming ringed with beautiful fat. The world was returning to her in bright pieces. They sat in a row on a bench, melting into it as dancing roller skaters zoomed past. Roller skaters! As if it weren't the impossible future, that ledge of time that fell off after the year 2001, but rather 1975 and she was a child again, set free from Kay for an afternoon.

When they got back to the apartment, it was dark, and Veronica had no idea what time it was. They took turns standing directly in front of the window box air conditioner to cool off. Then Ines, who wanted to renovate her kitchen, showed Veronica veined chunks of quartz and samples of gray soapstone. They marveled at the smoothness of the stones, holding the cold pieces up to their cheeks. When Ines and Art began to discuss the merits (Art couldn't see any) of a certain thousand-dollar Italian faucet, Veronica left them to their happy dispute.

When she got home, she threw her arms around John, nuzzling his velvety neck. Had she ever even *felt* skin before?

She told him; she'd still been in the habit of telling John everything. He was shocked and looked very young while he stared at her from the doorway of the bathroom. "You did *what?*" he asked, a look of confusion in his round eyes.

"We all did. I won't pump until—" He came into the room and leaned on the bathroom's double sink. She grabbed his hand and squeezed it. She tried to lace her fingers through his—how good that felt!—and he pulled his hand away.

"You're making it so much worse than it is. It's one night."

"You have a child. What if something happened to you?"

"But it didn't. I feel so much better." As she said it, her high started to fade, to pivot into regret.

"A child," he said again. "Did you forget? What kind of mother does that?" She was briefly aware of the double standard; he routinely went drinking with people from work even though he, too, had a child. She was not yet back to work. She was always at home trying to feed the baby. But she knew; she knew no good mother did it.

"I can never forget I'm a mother—don't you see?"

Two days later the heat broke; one night they had to put another layer on their bed. It drained her, stuffing the comforter into the white duvet so that they weren't clumped together. Such a gorgeous bed and Veronica still hadn't slept through a single night in it. John, who'd failed to help with the comforter, then offered to take Clara up to see his mother. "I'll go tomorrow morning and we'll spend the night. You'll sleep." The next night, she didn't sleep but met Ines at Adele's gallery, where the three of them took X before the opening of a video installation.

And there was one more secret time, with a bunch of Art's college friends. They'd driven up to the Storm King sculpture garden for the day, while John stayed home watching Clara and, Veronica guessed, playing Scrabble on his computer. The large oaks were beginning to shed their leaves, and Veronica laid in the grass as the autumn clouds collided overhead. Her pain evaporated. What she'd done was impossible, unthinkable. She was a terrible mother. But the problem (and the solution, in a way) was that each time she did it, she was whole, uncut.

One afternoon when Art and Ines were visiting—Ines was holding Clara awkwardly in her thin lap—Art blew the secret by casually referring to it. John reddened. Ines looked at Veronica as if to say that they'd reached the end of the experiment, that it was fun while it lasted; to Ines, John's feelings, the integrity of their little group—more like a family than any of their families actually were—was more important than any adventure. It was a relief that the whole phase was over just when it was becoming not only habitual but also savory, something Veronica had begun to look forward to.

In the red booth, she looked at Art for absolution.

"You're an excellent mother," he said. "You need to stop going in that direction."

"I'm mortified about the X." She was Winnicott's "good enough" mother, or she was horrendous. She was too attentive; she was too distant.

"We were experimenting and you liked it. A lot. It was only a couple of weeks."

A waiter came and piled up the thick off-white dishes. "But I had an *infant*. She was two months old!"

"Drink your water."

She did as she was told. "It's not who I wanted to be," she said, as Art slid one of his fat hands to her across the table. She gave it a perfunctory squeeze.

He looked at her awkwardly.

"Onward," she said, to relieve him of the pressure of her confidence.

"It was my fault," Art finally said. "We should have known you were . . . uh, in a state, I guess. With the new baby and everything. You can one hundred percent blame me, and John can too, if he's still mad about it."

She was simply too suggestible. She remembered the hospital's anesthesiologist, Todd, who'd administered the epidural. "All the moms love Todd!" a nurse had exclaimed, urging Veronica to get some pain relief. Jovial and muscular, Todd strode into the room but approached gently, like any guy eager to turn you on to a new drug.

"Thank you for saying that, but it was me. It's not you." John had had a glazed and distant look in his eyes as Art and Ines left that night. It was a look she recalled from their earliest meetings, of pure apprehension. He'd gone to bed angry that night, but she didn't stop him. She just wanted to go to bed too; each bit of sleep, however truncated, provided another chance, like a do-over granted in a children's game.

"You need to forget it," Art said, sipping his martini.

"It's getting harder and harder to forget." An ache tightened in her breastbone. "Nothing works. A drink. A nap with a good dream that is too short. You can't sleep as you used to. You're in some state of permanent vigilance. I'm not watching her now, but—"

"No, you're on vacation today."

Veronica laughed. "There is no vacation anymore!" She stood up and checked the contents of her bag, checked the ringer on her phone.

"Maybe you need a break," he said, then signaled to the waiter for the check.

A blast of cool air tumbled into the restaurant. She was drunk. Closing her eyes, an opening formed, like a rip in a black piece of paper with light coming through.

"Okay, I'll stay," she said.

In a few minutes, they arrived at the diamond district and ogled the faux diamond light posts on Forty-seventh and Sixth. White sleet drew down from the sky in thin sheets, startling against the blackened alleyways. A lone bearded man with tallis and curls walked by, like a specter down the long east–west block, his black briefcase no doubt stuffed with jewels.

"Where is everybody?" Art said.

"Wait, it's the Sabbath."

"Shit. It's Saturday. Why is it that the half goy knows this and I forgot?" It must have been close to four in the afternoon, because the winter sun hung low in the white haze. "We'll just check in with Abe Zelnick," Art was saying. "He might be there. I know he's not very religious. And then we'll go meet Ines. She's making us a reservation." Veronica watched the sun slide down in the west, like a pregnant woman sinking into a bathtub.

"It is all there already, Art. Clara has *ovaries*, all the eggs she'll ever have—they've been there since birth—a genetic arsenal, little half people stowed away for the future."

"Don't cry, V." she heard him say, as she fell with relief into one of Art's squeezes and the peachy orb of the sun slipped quickly beneath the horizon.

9

Saturday

John

In Derek's Corolla, the scent returned to John: sugar air, rum, white flowers. The very molecules that danced about his face and neck mingled with the pain in his skull. He closed his eyes on the way to Speightstown, knowing no one would object; *after,* moments of rest arrived unexpectedly, like dollops of whipped cream one hadn't asked for but could never refuse. The carful of people—Clara in his lap, Derek and Monika and Mum—murmured around him.

His face was starting to itch, prickly from missing one day with his razor. When he was twenty-five, when he only had to shave his face every three days, he'd teased Veronica about patronizing Glittering Sands. The resort stood sentinel on this island that had once—because of its location and its arable soil—been the center of the slave trade. Somehow Veronica's good liberal maternal grandfather and her timidly proud mother, who boasted of the several Quaker abolitionists in her family tree, had overlooked the history of the place. They returned again and again to the onetime English colony. John had defended Veronica while the Reeds, too earnest to completely condone a surrender to pleasure, criticized John for going on the trip with Veronica's family. They'd sent him off with a bitter autobiography about life on the island and the grim nature of its violent history.

Veronica had extolled the island's many virtues: the orchid jungles, the variety of indigenous animals, the cuisine, and even, she said, the plantations themselves if seen *as cultural artifacts* and viewed for historical and architectural interest. She had said she would not be made to feel like a terrible person for having come there. And John, in thrall to her completely, in a sexual haze, had agreed emphatically: She was a wonderful person. In the morning, as she walked bleary-eyed to the bathroom and peed with the door open, their subsequent talk was small again and not charged. When she returned to the bed, the sunlight slipped through the glass louvers like bleached swords, then danced around the shadows on their intertwined legs.

In the Corolla, it occurred to him: That very dance of light on breathing limbs must have been what Art had been talking about lately, what *happiness studies* was all about. Those mornings had been so great. He'd been happy. After their long waking chats, John would to rush back to his official room to shower, because David Edelson had called breakfast for eight-thirty sharp, and attendance was mandatory.

It was Veronica who had introduced him to, then steeped him in, pleasure. Even before Barbados, during their first winter together she'd returned from her family trip with a bottle of coconut oil from the island. When she'd cracked it open in her uptown studio, John saw that a thick layer of white cream topped the bottle. She'd massaged his shoulders, his hips, with it, and he hers. The same scent now permeated Derek's car.

Clara woke up and cried when they arrived in Speights-town. The air was full of shouts and the acrid odor of fish. John kept his eyes closed, as if he could live in a reminiscence of sex and coconut oil.

Once John was inside the clinic and lying on an examining table, Dr. Tisbury addressed him. Shoes squeaked on the linoleum in the clean pink room. The doctor pulled a white curtain around them.

"Tell me everything—John, is it?" Tisbury had an English accent. Pale-blue eyes stared wryly, and he pursed his lips as if he was containing something incredibly funny. He covered his mouth while the American spoke.

"If you could examine Clara first, I'd be grateful. She's had really bad diarrhea."

"Sure. Bettine, our nurse, will examine her, and you tell me your story. Tell me everything you remember."

The papered table crackled beneath him as he propped himself up on his elbows to speak. "I was sitting on the windowsill, looking at Lafayette. My wife was pretending to sleep."

"Lafayette? Is that your wife's name?"

"No, the *street*. In New York. It was snowing a little bit and I didn't *think*. I just got dressed." Dr. Tisbury jotted a note, then glanced toward Bettine through an opening in the white curtain; she raised one eyebrow as she adjusted Clara on her shoulder. "Please examine her right here, okay? Don't take her away."

"I'm taking her to her own table that is fresh," Bettine said authoritatively, placing Clara on an examining table to his right. Looking down, John saw that his own table was smeared with something dark: soil or manure or blood from his head.

"Mr. Reed, let's try again," Dr. Tisbury said. "I will ask you a few questions and you answer me as directly as possible." Tisbury asked John the year, the name of the American president, the month. John could tell he'd answered correctly by the lack of alarm or note in his questioner's gaze, but the words themselves—*2005, Bush, January*—were surreal. His words described a reality that still felt new, even fictional: The fact that Bush had snagged another election after stealing the first one, the reality of an unjust war. It struck him freshly: This was the context in which they lived. Large and small problems amplified one another, then settled stealthily around him, like gas enveloping his face.

Tisbury looked pleased. "In sum, you've not sustained a head injury of a certain type that causes lapses. That's good. Nonetheless, you seem a bit confused." Tisbury, fiftyish but young looking, had a playful air about him as if he truly liked John. It was a small but distinct comfort to be liked by a stranger. "Start with the injury and describe the pain you're experiencing, from the beginning. Start with *today* at Laura Simpson's."

And so, even though John felt as if he was getting way ahead of himself, beginning in the middle of the story instead of at the more logical beginning—his insomnia Thursday night, or the taxi ride on Canal Street, or the moment Veronica started reading aloud to him about obesity, or even when she was given the epidural and he'd had to leave the room—instead of beginning with the hysterectomy, or the first night home from the hospital, instead of beginning with pickup basketball with Arthur one night, when he'd insisted afterward that they go meet some girls he knew at the Corner Bistro, or instead of the bottle of coconut oil, which led to that massage. Instead of any of that, John told the story from the moment he'd arrived at Laura Simpson's, as arbitrary a beginning as that was. But once he began, like the reporter he'd been, he left out no detail, even recalling that he was leaning down to get a zwieback toast from the diaper bag when the ball hit his temple.

As he spoke, Tisbury smiled, amusement flickering in his steely English eyes. "This is all a very good sign. You're cogent." Next to him, to his great relief, Clara giggled with Bettine as a healthy-looking string of drool dangled from her lips. He watched as they gave her some sugary clear liquid for hydration. She licked the dropper greedily. "Clara's doing fine," Tisbury assured John when he asked. "The father is of more concern," he said. "You're severely dehydrated." Tisbury attached an IV to John's arm.

"The first IV is probably the beginning of the story, if you really want to know the truth," John said to Tisbury, as the doctor connected the plastic tubes to a bag of fluid. "Not this one but Veronica's."

Eventually Veronica had been put under completely. But at three centimeters she was still awake and John was essential

to her. "Let's walk," she'd said. "It's supposed to make it easier
to bear."

"Whatever you say," he said, kissing her forehead and
helping her stand up.

"Can you say that more often?"

They paced the hospital hallways, and she did this weird,
adorable thing where she leaned on him when she had a con-
traction, putting both hands on his shoulders and doing a plié.
It was ten at night and a whole day had passed since they'd
checked in to the hospital. She rolled her trolley of tubes. Her
doctor had forbidden drinking anything at all during labor, so
her lips had turned beige with thirst. John kissed her anyway.
Those moments when she leaned on him and gave way a little
at the knees made him feel useful.

Between contractions, life was normal; they strolled the
hallways of the hospital, chatting. "Look at that!" she'd said,
stopping. On the wall was a framed photo of an eagle soaring
over snowcapped mountains. The caption read, ACHIEVEMENT,
in bold letters.

"Wow," John said. "I always wondered where to get one of
those—oh my God, look." They passed another one. A muscular greyhound was running in a field of lavender. EXCEL-
LENCE, the caption read.

DETERMINATION, read a third, below an image of a boy reel-
ing in a large fish over a sun-streaked lake. "You know, Dr.
Berlin must have put these up herself," Veronica said.

John laughed. "No, hers says, 'power,' and she has it all over
her entire apartment, everywhere you look."

"Right, but what kind of animal is in hers?" Veronica
asked.

"A vulture," he said.

"Some sort of power elk," Veronica countered, and then they were in it together again, in that uncanny closeness. Was it odd to remember that institutional hospital corridor as a kind of heaven? They had been joking there together.

Across the room, Bettine sat with Clara, feeding her a bottle, and he wanted to object—it was probably store-bought formula. But Clara sipped with alacrity, cozying herself in the nurse's dark arms. Someone else was holding her and she was content. He wanted the three of them together again in the same room. He had to go home. But the head injury made his immediate departure impossible. Tisbury would return to observe him in two hours. He lay back on the papered table and focused on Bettine's singing, as he waited:

But I'm sad to say,
I'm on my way,
won't be back for many a day.
My heart is down,
my head is turning around,
I had to leave a little girl in Kingston Town.

10

Saturday

Veronica

On the subway, Veronica and Art sat next to each other. Veronica's leg was longer than Art's by several inches. "Ines wouldn't begrudge me one drink at the Oyster Bar," he said.

"You mean three." They'd just left the diamond district. At the first stop, the train screeched to a halt and the doors hissed open to reveal a throng of coltish girls too long for their skirts. She had been one of them once, giggling in a pack. Now she was solitary. "Are you drunk?" Veronica asked.

"Tipsy, I'd say." But Art's voice didn't waver.

"You'd never know it. How is it you can overdo it and then pop out, unscathed, and present a lecture the next morning?"

"That's just what I did at the Happiness Conference."

"I love that there is such a thing."

"I gave a lecture on the statistics of reported marital happiness," he offered. "Men report greater happiness levels after marriage, while women report a marked dip in happiness levels."

"A *marked dip*? How marked?" she asked, but the train became too loud again. Art was gesticulating, explaining something that she could hear only bits of, about reported happiness levels versus actual levels, about a margin for error, while the shocking data gnawed at her. It was distressing that happiness wasn't, by nature, reciprocal.

"It's not that they're *unhappy*, just that women always think they could do better," Art said as they reached the street. She buttoned her wool coat all the way up, but the wind went right through it. "Women don't accept things as they are," he said. "They want to change them."

"I don't think I've been unequivocally happy since I was first pregnant," she said.

"Are you sure about that? I remember you were pretty freaked out."

Veronica held on to his elbow as they approached an icy patch. "You know how anticipation is. I was happier thinking about the future." The future had arrived, and here she was, oddly enough, sliding along a patch of black ice with Arthur, her family gone.

"And you're happier with hindsight as well," he said.

"There was the mere expectation, the pregnancy itself, the huge mystery of it. Having no idea what would happen, what she would look like. I loved that."

"You were relatively quiet on the subject. Ines you can't get to shut up about it." He smiled and then stopped. "Well, until the test yesterday; now she fears the worst."

They'd arrived at the white-brick building, and Art led them past the ineffectual doorman, who looked as if he'd been installed in uniform in 1961. An older couple in very long parkas and galoshes joined them for a silent elevator ride. Arthur rang his own doorbell, his way of warning Ines he was not alone.

"You two were on a date, I see," Ines said as she opened the door and stood in the passage, rubbing a towel to her shampooed head. A damp floral smell billowed into the hallway. She smiled at Art and Veronica and then stuck out her tongue.

"We ran into each other," Veronica said, "and decided to get a drink."

"Hi," Art said, embracing Ines from behind as she tried to free herself.

"I can smell the alcohol—wow." Ines said, holding her nose. She looked at Veronica as she shoved Art away playfully. "You need to distract me," she added. "I've been going through the same bad test-result scenarios over and over again." Art kissed her cheek and she said, "Don't take off your shoes. I'm starving." She started lacing up her boots. "Is John back yet?" she asked, looking at Veronica.

"Nope. I assume Muriel has him wrapped up in some intense Evan worship and is plying Clara with oodles of educational wooden toys and they're fine."

"I thought he'd be back by now and booked us for four at Isabella's," Ines said.

"*What?*" Veronica blurted.

"What's wrong? You're tired of it?"

"No. Nothing." She hadn't even responded to Damon's

messages. He probably wouldn't show up at Isabella's. And if he did, seeing him might finally provide closure.

On the way to the restaurant, Veronica closed her eyes for a few minutes in the back of a cab. (It had been six hours since they'd started drinking, and she was tired.) To her surprise, a Rothko bloomed there, behind her lids, red and potent. She hadn't seen one in a long time. When she was seven, her father had taken her to the Rothko Chapel in Houston, David Edelson's hometown. They'd been staying with Veronica's grandparents for a few days during winter break, and Veronica could tell, as young as she was, that her father was uncomfortable with his parents, who smelled dusty, drank Sanka instead of real coffee, and stayed indoors with the air conditioner on, despite Annalena's repeated protestations: "It's a lovely day out and not actually too hot at all!" He didn't like their taupe ranch house, their small, self-consciously clean rooms with plastic seat covers, their bland roasts and crocheted doily toilet-seat covers. He didn't like their sterile modesty.

Every day he had to flee and do something extravagant, bring home fresh steaks from the expensive butcher or nice wine—his parents had one dusty bottle of Manischewitz—that he and Annalena could sip while they sunbathed behind giant aluminum reflectors. One morning he put Veronica and Annalena in the car and told them, "There is some culture here." They drove awhile to get to the surprise spot. When they arrived, Veronica noticed that her father did not get out of the car. He wanted to show his wife something refined, something interesting. He himself didn't need to see it; impa-

tient, fidgety, he was happier in the car toying with the radio
dial. Veronica heard him settle on "Best of my Love," as she
and her mother slammed their doors and made their way
across the lot to the chapel.

Inside the octagonal building were rows of benches like
those in the real chapels she'd been to with her mother's family.
On all sides were not pulpits but paintings. Huge canvases
from floor to ceiling, covered with somber grays. The paintings were boring. Her mother was always talking about
"exposing her to beauty." She took her to antiques auctions,
rare flea markets, and museums, missions that—because she
was really too young for them—always made her feel alone.
At first, the Rothko Chapel was the same; Veronica had to
watch her mother's absorption though she did not share it.
Annalena sat on a bench nearby and exhaled with the passion-
ate breath she reserved for colonial folk art. But then, almost
from the corner of Veronica's eye, something in the canvas
moved. She looked up, alert. The painting in front of her had
jumped. She stared at it. The paint undulated faintly, moving
away from her and toward her in waves. It was as monumental and frightening as the ocean. It was as mesmerizing and
unknowable. Annalena rose and took a seat on a different
bench, sighing heavily as if relieved of some great pressure.
Veronica called to her, "Mom, can we go now?" She was scared
of the silence that surrounded them, the air now tense and
kinetic.

Annalena, full of reverie since graduating from Winterthur, turned and raised a finger to silence her. "Be patient," she
whispered. "And you'll see. You may not ever come back
here." And so she studied Annalena's rapturous face. Giving

up, she looked back to the mammoth gray in front of her—there was nowhere else to look—and fell into it. Her fear petered out like it did right before she fell asleep. The hard bench beneath her fell away. She was not in Texas, she was not a daughter, she was not a girl, she was not herself; there was only this world of the painting and its tides, a subtle connection that she rode. She fell into time and space. She was removed—for that was how it seemed when her mother finally summoned her out and back to the car—and she was sure she had found something, an experience, a way of seeing, that was all hers.

Her grandparents died soon after, and David Edelson became fully a New Yorker, who never needed or wanted to go back to Texas. Her mother had been right: Veronica never returned to the chapel. But she often dreamed of the paintings and the feelings they'd produced, the disembodiment and that unnameable higher connection.

In the beginning of labor it was those colors, that undulation, that she felt along with the pain. Vision was transcendence, a gift. She had lived by this idea from the time she was six and all through her adult life. She had confided to John that seeing was the thing that made life good for her. If you could see deeply, if seeing could alter you, you were lucky.

After Clara, she could no longer see the same way. Their new world was comprised of bodily needs: Veronica was grounded in pain. Clara's hunger was continuous. And Veronica no longer had time to stare at a painting for very long. Instead, she stared at the baby's mysterious face. That face, whose every gesture and movement she strained to interpret, had become her chapel.

After, Veronica sometimes had dreams of color—zooming reds, electric blues—but when she woke up there wasn't time to see, only time to respond. She'd worried that, if you stayed in that dream, you might never emerge and reach another person.

Wasn't Annalena evidence of this encapsulation? But Annalena was not beyond convention; she did appear in the recovery room when Clara was born, bearing a large purple hyacinth.

"Sniff," she'd said, holding the plant close to Veronica's face.

"Hi, Mom," Veronica had said, overwhelmed by the cool earth scent of the flower.

"It's as if you can *see* purple when you close your eyes. How are you feeling?"

"Tired. The baby should be here in a minute. They're bringing her back from the nursery."

"I was worried about you," Annalena said, as she made room on the bedside table for the plant. A nurse shuffled in, holding the bundled baby, and Annalena watched as Veronica took Clara back into her arms.

"Do you want to hold her?" Veronica asked her mother after a few moments. She, too, wasn't beyond convention.

"I do. I definitely do," Annalena had said. "Look at her!" Yet she didn't make any motion to take Clara. "She's a stunner."

Veronica adjusted Clara's hat—her head was terribly coned from three hours of futile pushing—so her mother could see only the baby's face. Annalena reached out and touched Clara's cheek with a dry finger. Veronica shifted the pillow in her lap; the baby was too heavy on her incision.

The essential transfer, what she knew was supposed to

happen—the baby passing gently from her arms to her mother's, who had once held her—was not happening. Annalena clutched nervously at a strand of pearls around her neck, fiddling with the clasp. *Do you want to hold her?* Veronica had been foolish to even ask. She hadn't harbored hope as much as need. It was like wanting water in a desert. "Just look at those tiny eyelashes!" Annalena said, her blue eyes darting intently as she appreciated Clara's beauty; for Annalena, perhaps there was no higher calling than finding beauty. Veronica pressed the button in her hand, and a rush of morphine suffused her body. Almost right away, the awkward triangle softened.

They paid the driver and slammed the doors. Veronica tried to maintain attention as Ines talked about CVS versus amnio. "The prior can be done sooner, but it's much more painful and the results are not as accurate. Amnio is done later but tells you a lot very accurately. Why are you nodding?" Ines asked.

"Well, I did both, remember?" Both options were fraught in their own ways. She didn't know what to recommend. "What does Art think?" He was walking a few paces ahead of them.

"He's crazy and doesn't want to do either." Veronica's tipsiness was fading, but the image of a red painting dogged her, tempted her. How she wanted to dive into the moving tide. Images were encroaching now; the line between seeing and love was beginning to blur. But Ines needed advice, and Clara, in Irvington, needed the bottle in Veronica's purse.

"I guess I'm leaning toward the amnio," Ines said, pulling on one of her curls before tucking it back up under her thick hat.

"They'll probably make you do everything."

"I *like* everything, remember?"

Outside the restaurant, a tall man leaned against the side of the building with one long leg bent, his foot resting on the wall. Despite the cold, his white shirt glinted beneath his open coat. Damon. He wore no hat, and his bristly short hair looked almost platinum in the dark. He'd come as he'd said he would, regardless of her lack of response.

"What's wrong?" Ines asked, then followed Veronica's gaze. "Oh shit, the photographer." Because he had crushed Veronica, Ines had decreed she would never again utter his name.

"It's fine," Veronica said, a smile playing on her lips, wishing she'd suggested a different place to eat. For a moment, John's absence, Clara's distance, colors blurring, all of life, was supplanted by Damon; that old Damon soreness returned to her, like the secret spot where a tooth is loose that you have to keep checking over and over again. As they continued walking, she felt her face grow hot. Ines turned and looked at her sternly. "Are you okay with this?" Art had already ducked into the door of the restaurant to get out of the wind.

"I knew he was in New York, but I was going to ignore him. Do I look all right? Can you tell I've been crying?"

"*Have* you been?"

"I'm fine. I guess I just miss Clara." Damon was laughing on a cellphone, throwing his head back as if he'd never heard anything funnier.

"You were *crying*?" Ines said. "Get on a train and go to Irvington."

"It's too late." Veronica took off her wool hat and adjusted her hair. She made the mirror face, which she was embarrassed to see Ines notice.

"It is *not* too late. Skip dinner and go," she said.

But a force had begun, surrounding her, pulling her in.

"Oh no!" Ines said. "Do you want to go somewhere else?"

"You know what? I'm fine. This is good for me. It's been three years at least. It's sobering. This afternoon I was crying about my whole life for the first time in a long time; seeing him, I can compare now with then and see that even though I don't know what the hell I'm doing, I know more than I did *then*."

Ines squinted. "Liar."

A sort of bravado—she was not young and *totally* insecure anymore—seized her. She was a parent. Everything was possible. As she approached Damon, he looked up, and his face brightened. "You! My God. I'd thought I'd lost you forever. You look great!" He spoke as if they'd been separated against his will. He had always gushed when she ignored him. He grabbed her two hands with an old hint of propriety. His hands were so warm that she wasn't aware of her own reply, couldn't wriggle away, couldn't remember that she was now someone else, because with his hands he *did* own her. They stood there beaming.

"Hey," Ines said coolly to Damon, before she addressed Veronica. "I'm heading to the table. Meet me there." Veronica heard herself say to Damon, "Well, you should join us, because my husband isn't here and we have a table for four."

"I couldn't," he said, a faux demurral.

"Sure you could."

"I'll come say hi while I wait for my takeout." Damon put his hand on her back as they walked to the table, as if they were a couple, and then he cut it by saying, "My girlfriend is home with a cold, but she wants me to pick up some of their meatballs. Have you met Carmela?" He knew she hadn't. The name Carmela: It was as if he were dangling a piece of candy before her, a sweet caramel.

"I haven't met her, no, but I've had the meatballs. They're the best."

"And your husband, what's his name again?" Damon said, and winked as they approached the table and sat down.

She hit his arm because he knew. "His name is John," Art said, looking up from the table. Art detested Damon on John's behalf. This would be more than awkward, so Veronica pinched Damon's elbow, an old signal they had that could mean all sorts of things. She knew he'd get it. He would get her. Someone had to *get* her.

Thus prompted, Damon said, "Hey, Art, Ines. Veronica invited me to join you, but my girlfriend is home sick and I need to pick up the meatballs she likes, so . . ." He scratched the back of his neck as if he were abashed. "I should probably go."

"Right," Ines said. Art nodded.

"Are you sure?" Veronica asked, popping up, enjoying the automatic intimacy between them. "I'll walk you to the door."

When they stopped at the door, he looked at her, his gray eyes dancing. "I can tell your friends still adore me. I want to catch up with you, though."

"Me too."

"I have to wait for the meatballs," he added, as if to remind her that he was not *that* disappointed, and then he crushed her. "Once Carmela eats, she's always sleepy."

"Maybe I have met her—the food writer?"

"That's Constance." With Damon, there were always lots

of women. "Carmela has the worst cold. I'm actually heading over to the Parlour after, if you guys want to meet up for a drink—"

"Okay," she said too quickly. "I mean, I don't think we have any plans."

"What's-his-name is welcome to join us."

"Can you stop?" she said playfully. Shame consumed her; what's-his-name who was suddenly gone, what's-his-name whom she had spent all afternoon missing. For years she had counted on John. How had that sense of certainty been ripped away in one day? Well, he was not here, and Damon stood before her, playing with one of her hands, and there seemed very little to stop that melt-in-your-mouth sensation. "You don't even know about Clara, do you?"

"Clara," he said, almost delectably, as if he may have dated a Clara once.

"I had a baby—my daughter. She's six months old."

"Go get a picture," he commanded, and she went back to the table to get her purse. Ines rolled her eyes.

"Wow," Damon said when she returned. "I adore her. She's beautiful." They held the edges of the picture as if she were their child together. After some obligatory questions about the baby, he said, "Listen. So, so, *so* good to see you. You look— okay, I can tell you're not coming out later, but, like, email me or something, even though you're *married* and everything, and with a kid!" he said, as if being married in your mid-thirties were especially goofy.

She walked back to the table, safe. She imagined gorgeous Carmela, languid with a fever, craving meat as she sprawled on the couch in a silky white nightie. If Damon was out buying her favorite dish, they were in that first phase of infatuation he plunged into in the beginning, before he grew abruptly cold.

"Good riddance," Ines said as Veronica sat down.

Veronica said, "Yup," sort of quietly as she maneuvered in her seat.

"Why are assholes always named Damon?" Art asked, and then looked at Ines for confirmation. "It's true, or *Damien*. It means Satan in Latin."

Ines and Veronica ignored him and started looking over the menu.

"Of course, you always have *Angus* . . . as a name," Art continued. The two women talked about getting artichokes. Ines was hungry; Veronica wanted to get to another topic, to still the fluttering that made her want to race out the door and catch up with Damon. Ines and Art decided to split a salad.

When the food came, she checked her phone and found nothing. She abandoned her artichoke after a few leaves. She could not go to John. She wanted very sharply, for the first time, to hurt him. Her brief insight about seeing and love and how they could perhaps coexist grew muffled; Damon had nothing to do with love. He was stationed firmly in aesthetics, on the side of seeing.

His apartment was the same. Three cameras hung from hooks in the dark hallway, their huge lenses like trunks. There was a mess of newspapers and magazines on a glass coffee table and the red IKEA sofa where they used to fool around. He had one toothbrush and a tube of French toothpaste with Arabic letters on the back. Veronica opened it and squeezed some onto her fingertip. It tasted like licorice. She spread it around her tongue and gums. Her eyes were shiny in the mirror and she looked away. She was too fuzzy and wanted to be sharper. Art had ordered two bottles of red wine and Ines had abstained. After dinner her friends had promptly gone home, offering her the first cab, which she declined, saying she felt like walking a little bit. She watched them speed off; then she walked uptown. She could see the neon of the Parlour a few blocks away, and, as if in a dream, she had walked there. He'd been sitting alone when she found him, reading Friday's *Financial Times* by candlelight.

In a few minutes she would come out of his bathroom—ostensibly to see some of his new work—and they would kiss. That was all that would happen, a reminder of a prior life. She untwisted and smoothed her bra straps, cupped her hand over her mouth to check her breath, then sniffed her underarms. She smelled salty. His old tiles were clean, as if he knew that sodden ladies would sit here alone and stare at the grout before they fucked him, as if Damon, oddly domestic despite his itinerant lifestyle and dread of intimacy, had been in here during his time off with a tiny brush and a special grout cleaner from the hardware store.

She would go out and ask him about the tile grout to forestall the kiss. She cleared her throat for some reason, as if to protest, to say they really *shouldn't*, and then she took a deep breath. She was grateful for the smoothness of her shaved legs from that morning. Her shower, her bed, her daughter. She couldn't contemplate too much. How had John been completely silent for all of Saturday, the fattest day of the week, their day together as a family? Maybe they'd be home when she got back, fast asleep in their beds as if nothing had happened. Maybe something had happened to them. Panic made her breath stop. Recovering, she rinsed her mouth thoroughly and left the bathroom.

She sat down beside Damon on the red sofa. It felt very normal, as if no time had passed. She watched as he went to get a large portfolio by the door. He'd opened two more beers and placed hers in front of her on the coffee table. She stared at a color photo of two soldiers with machine guns standing under a huge amber chandelier. The crystals cast dappled shadows on their faces. One had a cruel smile, teeth like tiny knives beneath thin lips; the other stared ahead with a look of mourning at something outside the frame. "Where's this?" she asked. They were looking at pictures, nothing more.

"Baghdad." Damon sipped his beer and leaned back next to her. She could smell laundry detergent and smoke on his shoulder.

"It's remarkable. The tension between those two expressions. What is he looking at there, outside the frame?" She'd imagined some atrocity.

"You don't want to know," he said, then smiled. "He was looking at melted chocolate. I'd brought all these packages of M&M's, and when my assistant was opening one, we realized they'd melted. This soldier *really* liked M&M's."

When she looked up, he caught her face in his hands and kissed her warmly, then pulled away and smiled as if to gauge her reaction. Desire had returned. She kissed him back. Then stopped herself. "I have to go," she said, but when she stood up, he wound his fingers through her belt loops and yanked her back down.

"No you don't," he said, kissing the inner crease of her elbow. Warmth spread through her.

"I do. I'm leaving." But she was compelled by a delicate, burgeoning pull. "I can't do this."

"Sure you can," he said, drawing her onto his lap. She fit perfectly there. She was neither too small nor too big. He rubbed her back in warm circles.

"I cannot even be here right now. This is terrible," she said, as he nuzzled her chest and neck. She could stop then, after a few sweet short minutes in which her body was integrated, but she hesitated another moment and then another. She was no longer simply reassembled but was uncut.

"No, it's wonderful," he answered. And it was. "Stay," he said.

"I can't."

"I'm leaving in two days. I won't be able to see you again." He stroked the length of her thigh and looked truly sad. In two days it would be as if he had never been here.

"I'm so drunk," she told him, hearing her own preemptive excuse as she let him peel off her sweater and her tank top, and then, shivering but quite awake, she stayed. Very fast, they tore off their clothes. A part of her could see the stereotype; the rushed moves that both obfuscated and underlined what they were doing. He looked at her as he theatrically tossed his shirt over his shoulder.

This new energy was fragile, unsustainable, like a heart

beating in wax paper. She didn't dare open her eyes and take account of her surroundings.

The discrete motions—the kiss, the toss of the shirt—all linked together and something became of them. Then it was over. When they rested, she saw the long, unadorned window twinkling with lights and spires, the scarred wood dresser, her own blue bra. She wept a bit for the incontrovertible fact of what she'd done and for the closure. This was closure. Two distinct paths lay ahead of them. He would go back to Afghanistan, and she wouldn't walk through this door again. She had her answer. In his limited way, he did love her.

He didn't notice her tears as he breathed into her hair. He'd once admitted that he didn't like it when women cried, while John, oddly, seemed to welcome crying. John was good at comforting; Damon could not console, though he did ask, perfunctorily, if she was okay.

"I am." Relief, undeniable but brief, washed over her. Even after, she had always been herself, could still be herself. *Before* and *after* was a false distinction. There had to be a way to do this—to remain herself—and there had to be a way to change. He looked at her when she rolled to face him, understanding that she wanted him to refrain from saying anything at all affectionate.

Back in his bathroom, she rinsed off quickly, using a black soap from Jordan. She knew Damon would not tell anyone; he prided himself on his *discretion.* Their connection did not involve another soul. The event was in a parallel universe, and it was all hers.

As if abetting that dream of a parallel universe, a time out of time, the street was unusually light despite the dark sky above it. Ninety-fifth Street was a painting by Magritte. She touched her mouth, which was slightly abraded, and relished walking with a secret. A shudder ran through her. What had she done? It had felt inevitable. But it was not too late to go to them. It was not too late for everything. She rushed down the block, peering ahead for a cab. People were moving in cheery clumps up and down Columbus Avenue. She looked at her phone and was exasperated and grateful to find it completely drained of power. She would go to him; she could forgive John his startling departure, his absence. It was only eleven-fifteen. There was an eleven forty-five train to Irvington. They could all wake up together.

Saturday

John

Bettine was feeding Clara from a jar of pureed banana. A Gerber baby smiled comfortingly from the label. Tisbury had woken John—during the IV hydration he'd drifted off—and said, "Banana is a binding food, good for diarrhea."

It seemed that all of life was waking up and falling asleep over and over again. With luck, there was a dream in between, but the residue of this one was gone. His headache was muted and his daughter appeared content. She was recovering from an upset stomach in a foreign country, nestled in a strange woman's arms, and she was fine. Clara wasn't picky about her affections. What a gift! How had they not seen her resilience all along? They'd been too busy preening over her every move. He couldn't wait to tell Veronica how they'd been wrong. Clara was fine when they were not with her; she had an easy temperament, unafraid and trusting. He had no idea where this came from genetically.

Tisbury held a handful of blue pills. "I've given you a few of these for the pain, and I'll send you off with some extra." He poured the pills into a container. "Take them every four hours, precisely, *before* the pain returns."

He recognized the same painkillers Veronica had been given in the hospital. She'd liked them. "Thank you. Is this it? Can we go?"

"On your way. Your ride is waiting," Tisbury said, handing John a bill and then the baby. Clara felt solid and springy. She giggled when he kissed her cheek.

Derek was there, behind the curtain; Monika had vanished. "Monika had to go to work," Derek said, as if reading John's mind. "She's a masseuse at Turtle Cove. You going back to your hotel?"

"Lord Harrington's Castle? God, no. I need to go home. I need a phone. Mine's been dead all day."

"Okay, we'll get to one," Derek said, as John paid at the front desk.

As they drove out of Speightstown, Clara was happy, focusing intently, as she did after eating, on a shell she'd grabbed off the dash. She examined it from every angle, first with her fingers and then with her gums. John kept fishing it out of her mouth so she didn't cut herself, and she kept putting it back in. Derek talked about how hard it was to get a license to sell his work and about being an artist in the States; John could barely listen while tending Clara, until Derek said, "Maybe I could come visit you and your wife. In Soho, right?"

"What about Monika and the baby?" he asked, extracting the shell from Clara's grasp and letting her cry for it.

"You have a big place, don't you?" Derek asked amiably over her wail.

John laughed. Derek was probably imagining the home of someone who patronized Glittering Sands, and he was momentarily glad he was not that person. "No. I mean, it's not that big. It's all relative." He paused, recalling the glossy treacle spread of Lloyd Miller's duplex on Park Avenue. Derek had been so generous with him, but he just wanted to go home. He wanted to tell Veronica that he understood. He could forgive her. "Do you mind if I space out for a while?" he asked, to avoid refusing Derek an invitation to New York, and closed his eyes.

On vacation ten years ago, he and Veronica had existed on piña coladas and grilled cheese sandwiches at the golf club. But that wouldn't work anymore. Maybe it could work, maybe John could take her by the wrist and say, *When in Rome*, and she would get it. She would have to get it. She would have to buy Cheekies diapers and Pringles and regular baby formula. She could not have survived the thirty-hour labor and two surgeries to simply drift away from him, to shape-shift into a person who would eat only a farm-raised duck egg.

He opened his eyes as the car pulled to a stop.

"Clara seems like she's better," Derek said, when he noticed that John's eyes were open.

"I think she is," he said, sighing audibly with relief. "I need to call Veronica."

"Her mum?"

The drugs from Tisbury were kicking in and he felt no pain, only a vague panicky sensation, as if he were late for an exam. "Yes—wait, why are we going to Laura's? Can we go straight to the airport? I'm sure there's a phone there, and I want to get on the soonest flight possible."

"You're leaving today?" Derek clenched his jaw a little bit as he did a U-turn.

"You don't have to drive me there," John said, but Derek had already joined the stream of traffic leading to the new freeway. "Thanks for doing this," John added. They passed flowering trees, sugar cane, and cinder-block shacks on the sides of the road, punctuated by bright swatches of paint on some houses and by children—there seemed to be lots of children—playing in the dirty slits between the houses. Soon the domestic petered out, giving way to car dealerships and a massive grocery store called Rondo. John pictured Veronica picking her way through the aisles of Rondo in search of something fresh, something grown locally. Was this paradise? Hardly. He hadn't noticed when he'd arrived, but the island had changed radically in ten years. In the middle of a roundabout, a huge statue of a slave breaking free of chains faced the sun with a plaintive grin.

"We're going back to Mama," John whispered to Clara, his throat thick with tears. She took her little fat hand, shiny with drool, and batted at his mouth with it.

He wiped his mouth and looked out the window. But Barbados could no longer help him. Cars were everywhere.

Fluorescent trash danced in the gutter. Palm trees lined the roads, arching in mockery. Construction noise and dust surrounded them. The air was thick with a new smell that, at first, he couldn't place: burning garbage.

"She knows where you are?" Derek asked.

John hesitated before answering, fairly stunned by the familiar fear of losing Veronica. "She has an idea," he said. However erroneous, she did have an *idea*: Irvington. John's contrition mixed with dread. At this moment, Veronica might be speaking to Muriel, discovering that he and Clara were not there.

"She has an *idea*?" Derek persisted.

"She was sleeping when I left."

"You left her?"

"When you say it like that, it sounds like we were splitting up or something. It's not like that. She had a cold and hadn't been sleeping well lately, so I let her sleep in."

"You left with her girl, with her baby?" Derek turned and looked at him as he drove.

"Can you look at the road? No. It's not like that," John insisted, flattening beneath his own longing. He was in love with her. He would *never* leave her.

"Sorry, man, I don't mean to pry."

"No. No, you're right. Holy crap! I left." Derek didn't respond. John saw him play with the radio dial, the station mired in static. "I left her a phone message. She didn't pick up. But—fuck! I'm in a major rush."

"Monika would kill me," Derek said, accelerating, shaking his head as he spoke, then prodding further. "I take it you were in a fight?"

"Sort of. Jesus fuck!" John flicked off the white noise of the radio.

"Sorry, man."

"No, it's not you. It's me." He gave a guttural moan.

"I'll get you there, don't worry," Derek said, as he shifted gears and passed a large truck on the two-way road.

They stood on the curb amid several sealed white minivans purring with exhaust. In the distance, John heard steel drums jingling, drowned out by the planes overhead. In a blare of noise and that white-hot Caribbean light, Derek put his arms around John's shoulders and hugged him and the baby. "Wish me luck," Derek said. "Monika." And he gestured to form a huge belly on his skinny frame. He reached out and tickled Clara's chin with a long finger. She grabbed it and playfully hung on. She was fattened and mobile now, curling her spine around John's arms as if she might dive into Derek's, irrepressible in her need to explore. John adjusted her in his arms.

"Good luck, man," John said. "We all need it. And thanks." He took an old receipt from his wallet and wrote down his Crosby Street address and phone number for Derek. Maybe they would come. Maybe it would be better if they came. Hell, they should come right away.

Derek took the address and tucked it into his pocket. He said, "I don't mean to be a killjoy, but you can't go traveling with it."

"With what?" John asked, oblivious, bouncing Clara as he began to perspire.

"You don't want to go to a Bajan prison."

They stepped aside as people got in and out of cabs and John remembered; he fished the dime bag out of his knapsack and gave it to Derek in a handshake. Derek searched his pockets for the cash John had given him, but John refused it. "It's going to be great, this," John said, kissing Clara. "Monika, all of it." His eyes filled as if he might cry.

"Wait," Derek said, and pulled a stiff engraved card from his wallet. "Laura had her stationer make this for us." In black script, the card said their names and the London address they would be moving to after the birth. It was a card Annalena Chase Edelson would have deeply approved of.

"Fancy," John said, turning it over.

"You never know who's fancy," Derek said, and hustled back into his small red car. When Derek left, John felt an unexpected sting of abandonment. He wrapped his arms around the baby to try to quell it. Clara squirmed.

The last thing he remembered Veronica really wanting was her mother. It was after her "bag of waters" was broken, when the labor was still moving very slowly. "Can you call her?" she'd asked. The request caught him off guard. Veronica never admitted wanting Annalena. But when he looked at his wife, he saw that thin, solemn six-year-old trailing behind her mother at Sotheby's.

He left the room to call Annalena, and he asked her to come. "Oh, I'll wait at home until the baby's born," she said. Her voice was ashy and light as if she hadn't understood the request. There was a long pause. John sat in the meaty air of the cafeteria and considered what to say.

"She wants you here with her *now*."

"Well, I don't know what use I can be at the *actual* hospital. What can I do?" Annalena asked.

"She wants you to come. It's not that you could do anything."

When Annalena spoke again, she was halting, as if her reserve was melting. Her voice was breathy, almost shaky. "She's doing fine, isn't she?"

"It's been a long day—or, no, it's been two days—I don't even know how long anymore, and she asked for you." He heard Annalena laugh nervously in response. *"Just come,"* John said, surprised at the force in his voice, how her laughter had infuriated him.

She did arrive about half an hour later, looking small and scared, her mousy face emerging above a white blazer. She wore a red grosgrain headband. *Who wears a headband in 2004?* Ines always wanted to know. It was deliberately out of date, an announcement to the world that Annalena was not present.

"I brought some linen I'm embroidering for the baby. How is she?" Annalena said. They stood at the information desk on the maternity floor.

"She's hanging in there."

Inexplicably, Annalena had blushed. What the hell was she embarrassed about? "Should I wait in the lounge?" She gestured with the ridiculous linen sampler toward some seats. She didn't seem to understand that she was Veronica's *mother* and should not go anywhere. John resisted an urge to grab her tiny shoulders and shake her.

He took a deep breath. "No. Okay, um, no. You should

come *into* the room. Right away. I'm going in. Come when you're ready."

When he got back, Veronica was sitting in a chair as two people changed the dressing on her bed. She stood to let them peel the damp gown off her naked body and untangle it from the tubes, then put her and all her tubes into another fresh gown. Ignoring him, she moved back to the freshened bed, as if sleepwalking. He squeezed her hand when she was settled. She opened her eyes. "Where's my mother?"

"She's here, honey," he said.

"Where?"

"She's in the lounge."

"Why?"

"She said she's not sure what she can do in here."

"Did you tell her I need her?" she asked, tears streaming down her face.

He'd failed her; he had failed to bring her the one thing she had asked for. Why had he not forced Annalena into the room? "I did. She has some, um, sewing she's doing, but she's here in the building. She's—she loves you," he blurted, desperate to comfort her. Veronica's eyes lit for a moment; then she hid her face as if ashamed. She turned and faced the wall.

"Your mom is here for you."

Veronica did her best to curl her ungainly body into a fetal position. She pulled the covers up to her chin.

"I'll ask her to come in again," John said, but it was futile. He felt his wife's disappointment. What could he do about it? Wanting Annalena wasn't rational. She wasn't a woman who could be had.

"Don't you get it?" Veronica said. He'd become the despised

messenger. And then the door opened tentatively. Veronica sniffled and looked up with expectation. John felt a wave of relief before Muriel's face appeared in the doorway.

The two-fifteen flight to JFK had already left. There were no more flights until the next morning, an eternity and a thousand dollars later. He looked around the airport aimlessly, as if there'd actually be anyone to help him.

As a child, he'd been lost once at Wolman Rink around Christmas. Bravely he'd circled the ice, then went around again. Couples zoomed past. Bits of ice sprayed into the air. Next he tried staying in one place, to see if his parents would appear. Eventually it was too cold to remain outside. He found his parents in the café, cooing over Irish coffee. When he appeared, they asked casually if he wanted to taste it. *But I was gone*, he wanted to say. He'd sipped the fiery drink and it scalded his throat. He was then offered a hot chocolate. Perhaps only a few minutes had passed, but in the time he'd been missing, unnoticed, a desert had expanded in his chest. He'd stood alone on the ice, the crowd of skaters zooming past. The loss was his alone.

He wanted to call Derek and looked at the engraved card; it listed Derek's London number only. In the cacophonous airport, he was homeless. Clara was hot and cranky.

"Dadooooo!" she babbled loudly, with anguish and tears in her eyes. Little red huts sold refreshments and souvenirs in the impossibly bright sunlight. Even in the late afternoon the sun was unrelenting. It was an amazing thing to have a home. To be able to go there and take off your shoes and put your keys down on the counter.

John went to one of the huts and ordered a Banks beer and sat at the bar, holding the cold bottle against his hot forehead while Clara wiggled. She arched her tiny back and grunted stiffly, wanting to be set free, then leaned down as far as she could toward the ground. How he needed to keep her from that ground, where she might eat the cigarette butts and *lick* the floor.

He bought two of the squat Caribbean bananas from a pruned woman selling them off her head. He fed Clara some from his fingers, which helped somewhat, but then she flapped her arms and feet frantically, wanting more. He bought fried chicken at one of the little huts, eating it himself and giving Clara a bottle of goat milk. When she was calmer, he set out again—he had to, for he was *her* home—over the hot tarmac to a white stucco airport motel.

1 2

Saturday

Veronica

Veronica was back at Grand Central for the second time in one day; it made her feel homeless. Her bra dug into her back in the way it did when she was overtired, as if her body were melting. The train ticket was in her hand. She stood eagerly on the platform. Soon. Soon she could hold Clara, the baby's body draped warmly over her chest and shoulder. She and John had joked in the early weeks after Clara's birth that they wanted to take turns being put into slings, rolled into flannel blankets, and carried in each other's arms. It was one of the tragedies of adulthood: that one was simply too large to be lifted by another person.

John *had* supported her full weight once during early labor. She would have to remind him: Pain was something they could get through together. She'd been so alone, but she needn't be anymore. They needn't be alone.

Nearby, a teenage couple, underdressed in matching blue fleece, waited near the track, kissing. The boy held the girl's face with both hands as if it were breakable.

On board, Veronica unwrapped and ate a very useful egg sandwich—it had been so long since she'd last eaten from a diner—and had a coffee. No, it was not a farm-raised duck egg; no, it was not a fair-trade macchiato. The cheese on the sandwich was a bright yellow American square. The bread was not whole grain but white and fluffy as a cloud. Mendelsohn's wife, Jamie, would be appalled. But the sandwich was so good. It was *greasy*. Had anything ever felt cozier than the egg sandwich and her own window seat on this train? She had a good view across the aisle, where the young couple in fleece had planted themselves to make out. And she enjoyed it—yes, she liked seeing the happiness of others, as if in John's absence she had suddenly become, or was perhaps *once again*, magnanimous. She wasn't sure why, but she felt wiser, seasoned, and even a little taller.

The teenage girl caught Veronica's eye and blushed. Veronica actually winked. There she was, an entirely new incarnation, an older woman capable of dispensing affirmation and comfort.

The train rumbled through the Bronx. She watched a man across the aisle from her as he dozed off—he was a boy, really, stuck inside a pin-striped suit. John, too, was simply a boy. It seemed perfectly understandable that John had had no answer for her about the reasons for her hysterectomy. Was there truly a dangerously low level of amniotic fluid? Was it really necessary to induce labor? In the intervening months he'd failed to come up with an answer. But how could he have? And how could he or she *ever* know if things might have happened differently? Life after the birth had been *a lot*; it had all been a lot for John too.

She licked ketchup off her thumb, aware not only of the high-fructose corn syrup that was its main ingredient but that John had felt helpless. The man in the suit awoke with a start and pulled a slim cellphone from his pocket. He stared at it with apprehension, then hope.

She would never have another child.

But as she sat on the train, the reality of Clara finally *eclipsed* that fact. Clara was a baby and would be a girl and might someday make out with a boy on a train. She would sneak out of the house at night and have a life Veronica wouldn't know about.

The young couple kissed, but the girl kept looking at her watch and giggling as the boy lunged for her. The faint odor of skunk slipped through the doors at one station: The city was receding, growing distant. Crosby Street seemed like another continent; the loft, a mere stage. The skunk odor grew stronger. There were animals in the woods, doing their animal things; there were trees and crackling branches and warm houses, perfuming the air with wood smoke. There was no parallel reality, no other way things could be. This was it; a single cold night in January. She had betrayed John. She would not tell him, but the fact was there, for her to know and to live with. Soon she'd see his house, the small Tudor one he'd grown up in, with the modest boxwoods and the amazing climbing tree. She had the comforting but also unsettling sensation of moving backward through time. She was almost there.

1 3

Saturday

John

The inside of the new hotel room was stucco like the outside, a white cave of rough walls, and Clara wailed within it. John held her and paced, and this quieted her somewhat, but if he dared to stop she screamed. He longed to be free from her, to be alone. There had been that moment of morning glee as he dressed her for the beach, that sense of his own ability. He'd considered himself pretty capable as a father, but he was realizing now that he hadn't spent very many consecutive hours alone with her. He had scoffed at Veronica's fatigue. He had not fully believed it. She had been recovering from surgery, been post-partum, and had begun working full time. She spent almost all of her free time caring for the baby. His smudged reflection in the dirty mirror above the dresser showed that he was now experiencing a small fraction of her fatigue.

Clara screamed directly into his ear. The sound of a baby crying was considered torture; tonight he understood why. Tisbury's drugs were wearing away. His head was beginning to pound. He hugged Clara, saying, "Daddy's here," and feeling totally preposterous. To wish your child asleep, to yearn for her to sleep more than anything else in the world, was the plight of parenthood.

The sleep-training book they'd consulted when Clara was four months old had called letting the baby cry it out *extinction*, with no irony at all, with no admission that crying it out *was* a little death. Veronica and John hadn't been willing when Clara was four months old, but they were planning to try it soon. In that stucco room, in a guilty reversal, John held Clara and rocked her, all the while wishing for *extinction*. Time thickened and stretched. A spiderweb dulled the plastic leaves of a fake plant on the dresser. Clara's body grew heavier as he paced. He paused to examine the bruise on his forehead in the dresser mirror. A swollen purple lump muddied his hairline where he'd been hit by the ball. Clara began to scream, so he resumed pacing, his biceps aching. The bedspread was white chenille, the pillow mustard foam beneath a thin pilled cover. Finally Clara's eyes almost rolled back in her head with exhaustion and closed. They snapped open once more—no!— and then shut.

He waited a full fifteen minutes and then carefully, in a ridiculous mime of slow motion, placed Clara on the center of the bed. When he was sure she was down, he picked up the hotel phone and dialed his home number. Two hours had passed since Derek had left him at the airport. He had a tic in one knee that was trembling. He had to reach Veronica; it was a relief to get the machine.

"Hi, it's me?" he said, his intonation like a question. "Um . . . I'm on my way home. I should be there by . . . tomorrow, Sunday, by one, maybe more like two. I—I'm sorry I missed you. I mean, I keep missing you. Okay, see you soon. I'd put Clara on, but she's sleeping. Okay—bye." Despite his relief, he wondered where she'd gone. They never went out two nights in a row.

He worried that it was too late: Ines must have told Veronica about Barbados. Or, and maybe this was worse, she had gone to Irvington. He stood up, paced the darkening room, and then dialed Irvington. His old number, the one he'd memorized in middle school, made him nostalgic. Muriel and Evan announced themselves on the machine. Why had his mother not changed the message? It had been nearly a year. The recording stopped and he breathed into the space after it, unsure what to say. Exhaustion pivoted to confusion. He hung up.

Last he called Veronica's cell. His stomach lurched when he heard her voice mail; she was someone who answered phones— they'd always shared this quality—who, despite all the technical deferrals to connection available, wanted to hear real voices, who always kept phones fully charged and ready to connect.

Failing to reach her, he forced himself to lie down— gingerly, so as not to wake Clara. Outside, machinery hummed on the humid ground. Through the window he could see a rickety dolly overloaded with suitcases being wheeled across the tarmac by a man who looked too old for the job. A red duffel bag tumbled off and was left there; for several minutes, no one noticed or came to pick it up. For some reason, this gnawed at John: the stranger's loss of hair gel and bathing suits and the possibility that they might never be recovered.

There were at least eight people in the operating room. Later, there'd been an entire additional body, twenty-one inches from head to curled toes in his arms. The nurse who was restocking the cabinet didn't understand natural selection. How could these people have been entrusted to bring life into the world, to save life, when they failed to understand the concept of evolution? Clara had looked like John, and he was her protector. He'd held her there when the alarm sounded and an orange light flashed on her tiny pink hat. The woman who was restocking the cabinet dropped a box and ran to the orange light, to the room where Veronica was hemorrhaging. There was something primal and also futuristic in the rhythmic noise, the sound of an emergency. He was now a father. The family he'd come from was gone. His sister was overseas; his father was dead; his mother remained, circling a poorly heated stone house alone. How innocent Veronica and he had been to presume they could make another family. It was not something you could plan or count on but merely a happy accident. The orange light continued its assault, burnishing the dry white space. Abruptly, the alarm stopped. Veronica had not yet held her daughter. Maybe she never would.

He told himself he should sleep and he did for a while, the foul dreamless sleep of passing out. He woke perspiring heavily.

Clara was whimpering. He picked her up and she howled. His head throbbed. Her body was too hot and also clammy to the touch. Her eyes remained closed as he tried to soothe her, but she was in a nocturnal rage, kicking and thrashing as he tried to contain her.

Giving her a bath did not work. Wrapping her in a towel made her incensed; extinguishing the air conditioner enraged her. With each of his attempts to calm her, she expressed her extreme frustration with him, as if his willful good spirit, the fake cheer of a parent trying to calm a child, was wearying to her. Finally, he understood: She was hungry. She was very hungry. It had been four hours since she'd eaten and she was usually asleep by this time, but her wails were unmistakable. He fed her some Bajan formula—the goat milk had gone sour—and she was sated for an hour. Then the whimpering began again, a mournful sound drained of energy. The air conditioner had been on for a while and the room was cool, but Clara was hot. She was burning up. He gave her the medicine from the dropper and she greedily licked the sugar, then cried when he took it away. The fever broke in half an hour, but he looked at the bottle of medicine doubtfully. He would barely have enough to keep her fever down if it continued through the night and the next day.

The few hours after she was calm peeled away until morning. She rested, then clung to him, alternately sucking vainly on his hand and clenching down hard on his fingers. He'd had little sleep; no dreams. The thin smell of exhaust permeated the cell-like room, as the heat of the sun increased. Clara lay limp in his arms as he hurried out to catch his plane.

PART THREE

NEST

1 4

Saturday Night and Sunday Morning

Veronica

The clean, easy commuter's step off the train, that danger-ously wide gap between the car and the platform, delighted her. Off she flew, buoyed by the egg sandwich and the teenage lovers. The town itself, its extreme cleanliness, the perma-nence of its Wing Cleaners and Stride Hardware, flooded her with nostalgia. The now-stronger skunk smell had been hov-ering there for a decade, since John had first introduced her to his family; she had become his family. Yet as Veronica walked down the steps to the lone taxi, she noticed her hair was still damp from Damon's shower. She got in the taxi and leaned forward to tell the driver the address.

The young couple in blue fleece stood on the platform under floodlights and kissed goodbye; the girl pulled away first, offering him a handshake, which made them both laugh.

After this strange night, vision was returning to her again, as it hadn't for months.

The driver took Oak and then turned uphill onto Willow. They passed John's Georgian brick elementary school, the soccer field and seesaws, and then the brown shingle house with its legend of a suicide. Beside her in the dark, another cab carried the man in the pin-striped suit from the train, who was squeezing the bridge of his nose.

She would console John. She had changed but was not devoid of memory. The October before Clara was born, they'd had a tiff at the community garden on East 2nd Street when Veronica had wanted to go to eat with the vegan gardeners at somebody's apartment and John had whispered, "It's going to be terrible. Trust me. The whole thing reminds me of my parents' awful potlucks in the seventies," an analogy that had only intrigued Veronica.

"But I've never been to a potluck," she quietly persisted. "They're farming on a roof in the East Village! How amazing is that?" She held a pamphlet about the collective's fall harvest and gazed up at the third-floor rooftop where she imagined the last of summer's overripe yellow tomatoes dangled above Second Avenue.

"You go alone if you want. I have work to do."

She kissed his palm. "But I want to be with you."

They were startled by a clap of thunder. It started to rain. Without discussing it further, they hopped into a cab and slammed the door. John gave their home address. Veronica glared at him. She simmered for a minute, then looked out onto the blur of the Bowery, letting it go. He wrung his hands, as he sometimes did, but then one hand sort of fell into her lap and idled there, lolling between the silk skin of her bare knees.

They'd kissed silently throughout the ride. They'd had to say nothing, mute as they were with lust, as they pushed their way into the cramped Crosby doorway, into the small elevator and the apartment itself, finally lying down on the Tibetan rug.

Rain gushed in through the open windows, soaking the freshly painted sills. Earlier the same day, she'd experienced an odd twist within her, an aching little pop on the right side of her belly, and knew, since she'd been waiting for such a thing, that she'd ovulated. The conception was that deliberate *and* that accidental.

The storm, the broken late-fall heat, the difference of opinion, had created their daughter. Maybe if it hadn't rained that night, forcing them into that backseat, if the weather had remained humid and stagnant and they'd walked instead or eaten with vegans, but they hadn't.

They'd held each other for a long time before separating, and they'd been happy and had drunk some white wine in little water glasses while they lay on the rug. A fluttering haze sifted through her whole body like a purr. She'd never felt anything so dynamic and fleeting as the very first moments of conception.

"Can you really feel something like that?" John had asked. His eyes remained serious; his smile betrayed his skepticism.

"I'd like to think you can," she'd answered.

He didn't question it again.

In the chilly cab in Irvington, she watched the tree air

freshener spinning from the rearview mirror; she had done something that jeopardized everything.

The taxi progressed uphill to the Reeds'. Nine months after that rainy, fateful night, when she had finally been pushing, Muriel's face appeared in the doorway, a reminder that her own mother would not come in. Annalena had been embroidering somewhere, Veronica had been told, some tight concentration of threads that only she could see the beauty of. It would be a comfort to see Muriel now.

The cab pulled into the Reeds' driveway. Muriel's pearly-white hybrid was parked nearby. Veronica paid the driver and closed the door, shivering in the crisp night.

She crunched her way over the gravel drive, trying not to make too much noise, because it was late, already twelve-forty-five, and the house was sealed and darkened for the night. At the front door, she considered knocking but refrained. She didn't want to wake them up. In the thin winter air, she inhaled with relief: Clara with her oat–almond sweetness was inside, asleep.

She checked the back door, searching under the mat for a key, but there was none. Making her way to the side of the house, she decided she'd climb through the window. She crossed the backyard, where John had told his parents he was leaving his career as a journalist. She hadn't been entirely sure of his decision—he was doing well as a writer—but she wanted him to be happy. Someone else's happiness—his and then, later, Clara's—had become as important as her own.

She had betrayed them in the individual days, sometimes only in a minute here or there, in the months of her frequent absence. But tonight's singular event was, if not entirely accidental, perhaps *necessary*. It was Damon who had revived her passion and her perspective. He had returned her to John.

It was hard to open the living room window. Muriel had put the storm windows on and they'd frozen in place. Veronica pushed with all her effort, grunting a bit in the cold. She looked up to John's window and imagined the outline of the portable crib aligned near his old twin bed. She threw a pebble up at the window, a gesture from the movies. Nothing.

She pressed her knees together, then, desperate, undid her jeans and let urine steam into the snow. Finished, she moved around to the back of the house to what Muriel called the "sunroom." She easily pushed in one of the screens on the porch surrounding it and then opened the door to the living room, which Muriel often went in and out of to get firewood.

The comforting woody smell was in the house, and a small ember spit in the fire. Later she'd wonder why she hesitated. After two interminable days of waiting, she didn't run up the stairs. Instead, she lingered there in the sunroom on a wicker sofa, reading about heirloom tomatoes in an ancient issue of *The Learning Annex*. Soon she would get up to take a peek at John and Clara, and then she'd sleep on the sofa with the wood smell. They could discuss everything tomorrow, why he had not called, what he was truly angry about. She flipped through to the end of the leaflet, and then it hit her.

She catapulted herself to the stairs and mounted them quickly, then moved down the hallway past her own wedding portrait, in which she'd smiled so hugely her face looked like it might break, for she had known, finally, what people were talking about when they said they *knew* someone. Heart pounding, her hand on the knob, she entered John's boyhood room.

Gray shadows danced above the white Lucite built-ins on the far wall. The twin bed was smooth, royal blue, and unruffled. She scanned the room quickly for the crib, as if it might be tucked in a corner, the baby sleeping safely inside, but the room was empty. She took two steps back into the hallway, where the grandfather clock ticked loudly. Incredulous and tearful, she went back into the room and opened his closet, as if to find not him, not Clara, but some sign of who he was. Who was he? Nothing but a faded *Betty Blue* poster secured under a plastic basketball hoop peered at her from inside the door.

Sleepless, Veronica had risen from the couch at some unknown hour and rummaged through the powder room for some of Muriel's melatonin. There was none. Instead, she opened her purse—the giant purse held everything—and found a sample from Lancelot Drugs, John's new sleep aid that was still in trial. She swallowed one of the blue pills without water. Waiting for it to kick in, she paced the living room, pausing to pick at the wax in a dark-green candle. She decided she couldn't wait, even if she was going to wake them up, and called the apartment—they must have crossed paths; she and John must have been on two trains heading in opposite directions at the same time—but she got the answering machine. There was one message from John saying he was on his way home and sounding faintly desperate and out of breath. The phone in her hand, Veronica lay down on the couch and drifted off to sleep.

In the morning, she heard Muriel padding down the stairs. She rose from the sofa, fixing her tangled hair with her fingers and wiping her eyes. They met at the foot of the steps. Muriel screamed.

"I'm *so* sorry, forgive me," Veronica said, and reached to embrace her mother-in law.

"What are you doing here? I mean, I don't mean it like that, but you scared me!" Muriel wore a hot-pink velour robe and drew a thin hand over her breast. Her shoulders trembled.

"I didn't mean to frighten you. I got here when you were asleep." There had to be an explanation. Muriel had to know where John was.

"Oh gosh, no, I mean, I wasn't expecting you. What are you doing here?" Muriel said. "When did you get here?"

"John didn't tell you . . ." Veronica began, but it was now clear he'd never been here.

"Is everything okay?" Muriel asked.

Veronica lowered herself to the foot of the stairs. Her head was thick and gauzy from the sleep aid, her speech slow and deliberate. "No. I don't know. What time is it?' The air seemed cosseted, lined in cotton. They were miniature figurines inside a dollhouse.

"Noon already. Just past."

"Oh my God." She hadn't slept this late since high school.

"I've been awake doing the crossword," Muriel said. She fluffed her gray hair, assuming the role of the strong one as Veronica wilted. She stood up and fell into her mother-in law's pink caftan, her lanky but totally secure arms. She looked up into Muriel's face and saw John's light-brown eyes, so similar that she even recognized the same black fleck in the left one. The uncanny miracle of heredity.

"Tell me everything," Muriel said.

So Veronica told her about Friday, about the note, the nap, the terse affectionate messages, and then about Saturday, with its disquieting silence. Veronica looked up to Muriel, still somehow believing that this woman, a born nurturer, a teacher of small children, would have an answer for her.

But Muriel's sudden rush, her air of emergency, her total ignorance about their whereabouts, scared Veronica. Quickly, Muriel went to the kitchen, rummaging for the car key, while Veronica—still groggy from the effects of the sleeping pill— followed and stood at the butcher block, trying to decipher a Metro-North train schedule. "I think he went to Massachusetts, to Amherst. He must have. He's had this weird idea for months of visiting his alma mater and taking the baby with him."

"Do you think so? No, no, dear," Muriel said, snatching the train schedule. "I'll drive you home. Get dressed."

"I am dressed. I'm so sorry to bother you."

"Don't be silly." Muriel spoke with a refreshing harshness she rarely employed. "It's not a bother."

As Muriel ran upstairs to get dressed, Veronica looked through the picture window to the backyard. A squirrel skid- ded over the icy deck, then bounced up to a branch, where it began to eat, oblivious to the cold. Amherst was it. Some yearning John had for nature, to escape the city like Thoreau and let Clara see *clean* snow.

"Could he be with Arthur?" Muriel ventured as they moved outside to the car.

"No, I was with Arthur and Ines last night. They thought

he was here too." She looked at Muriel, as if she might say something to change that reality, but Muriel only reflected her worry, her face a mass of lines.

By one P.M. they were sitting in her baby whale of a car, driving silently, as hybrids do, over the winding roads, through the quaint town, past the brown depressing house, to the highway.

On the Saw Mill Parkway, Muriel mused, "Once when he was about three he got out of bed in the middle of the night and went over to the Sandlemans' to play. He just waltzed across the street!" She laughed at the memory. How was she even capable of smiling? "You have no idea how frightened I was to see that empty bed." He was once Muriel's baby; she would always find him endearing, no matter what he did.

After that, they drove in silence. Veronica recalled the details of John's boyhood room. Everything in that room had once moved her, making her feel, as love does, that she had known him all her life. Yet she was not his mother; her love was conditional.

Her romance, her memories, her real diner coffee on the train, her sudden compassion, all felt flimsy and foolish.

Muriel touched her, laying a hand on her knee. The tenderness surprised Veronica—no one in her own family touched a person who was upset—yet she did not push her away.

"Thank you," Veronica said, as the two women entered Manhattan, rolling into the scant Sunday traffic of the Henry Hudson, where a faint light presided over the dirty slush.

1 5

Sunday

John

Whenever there'd been a discussion of the equator in school, John had envisioned a visible red line, a hot ribbon wrapped around the center of the earth. The parts of the globe that were green were land, and the parts that were blue were ocean. Once an image fixed in his mind, he was stubborn about it, argumentative with his gentle mother as she tried to show him the nuance of things, the way reality was not as he had imagined.

Sunday at dawn, Clara had taken a full bottle of formula and had terrible hiccups. Her fever seemed to be returning as the daylight intensified. The sun was already white and aggressive on the baking tarmac. As they walked across the hot runway, he wouldn't have been surprised to see that red line burning their path. In the airport's small pharmacy he asked for more medicine, but the saleswoman laughed and explained that the pink liquid was "an American luxury." She smiled indulgently as she eyed the empty bottle and explained that they did not have any in Barbados.

With dread, he mounted the stairs to the plane. With each step his head crashed, metal against bone. He hadn't been able to take the painkiller on time, as Tisbury had advised—now he was waiting for water to swallow it—and the hammering was ceaseless, overwhelming. Clara faced out in the carrier and kicked repeatedly; she seemed to have her mother's long legs and knocked her little heel into his crotch.

Don't feel sorry for yourself, Evan would've said.

Take the medicine without water, Muriel might suggest. But he wanted simply to complain. Complaint raced in him like something wild. If Veronica kissed him, if his own wife still wanted him, he'd vow not to complain anymore. Although wasn't the option to complain to your beloved essential? Veronica had complained to John for months: the insensitivity of the doctors, the numbness of the incision, the mood shifts from the hysterectomy, the sleeplessness of life with an infant. The world, life, *not* as it should be. He'd complained too. They'd indulged in grievances small and large. They'd complained so much, they no longer heard each other.

He wanted to say to her, *I know,* wanted to listen to her as Ines and Art must have during their weeks of "experimentation." Clara's small forehead was heating up. He had left Veronica. He had taken the baby. Derek had said, *her baby,* and, yes, Clara was irrefutably hers.

His mouth was parched. The stewardess approached eventually and offered him water. He swallowed the overdue pills with gratitude and told Evan that Veronica had needed to do what she did those fall weekends and not to judge her, that he had been utterly consumed with work and had not been there for her, as she would have liked him to be. He had not been there for her.

Evan would've said, *Your mother and I can see a few too many glasses of wine every now and then, but really.*

He wanted his dead father to stop talking and Clara to stop jumping on his lap. He turned Clara around to face him and she sneezed on him. Wiping his face on his sleeve, he tried to change her diaper right there in the seat—it was only urine—and with a smile, she slid a tiny finger into his nostril. His large-pored, repulsive man nose. A flight attendant saw and smiled. If he could hand Clara to her, to anyone, well, then they would see how hard it was. He balanced Clara's half-nude wiggling body on his knees and removed the soaking sack of diaper. Charitably, the flight attendant waited and reached to retrieve the Cheekie. Seconds ago he'd felt capable of hurting the baby, but once she was dry and calm, he felt he would *kill* anyone who harmed her.

The five-hour flight continued, full of impossibilities: loose stool creeping up her diaper onto her back just when the fasten-seat-belt light went on; her recurrent shrieking and twisting as she gnawed on a magazine, stood on his legs, and tugged at the fascinating silvery hair of the passenger in the seat in front of him. Her energy, even with a fever, was constant.

"Karma!" he accidentally said aloud.

"Excuse me?" said the woman beside him. She was young, maybe twenty, with light caramel skin, very long eyelashes, and too many bracelets decking both wrists. She looked at him warily.

"Are you . . . uh, going to New York?" he asked her.

"Yes—obviously," she said.

"Do you live there or are you just visiting?" It was Arthur who counseled that small talk put people at ease.

"I live in New York," she said in a monotone, with an unmistakable New Yorker's detachment. "I was visiting my family."

"It's a beautiful place—Barbados—isn't it?" Perversely, he continued to speak. He straightened the baby's sock as if he felt at all normal. As if he were a nice normal older man, a father.

It was disconcerting to see that she didn't buy it—his normalcy, that is—and lifted a magazine to block her face. He stared as one can on planes at parts of her, the smoothness of her wrists, the youthful skin of her collarbone and chest. Blemishless.

Art had once described Veronica this way after he and John first met her. *Blemishless*. Art had said nothing like this about Ines, whom he'd met at the West End up by Columbia months earlier, although he had clearly liked her too. It was after one of their basketball games on West 12th Street, and Art had let John shower at his tiny studio on Jane Street. They were meeting the two women at the Corner Bistro for a beer.

Art skipped a little on the way to the Bistro. He was still a grad student, but he seemed already focused on practical routes to happiness (as no graduate student, it seemed to John, ever was). John asked him about his parents as they walked. Art had mentioned the furrier and the housewife, humorously but without derision.

"Whatever they *were* or *did*," John said, "they clearly loved the shit out of you."

"Of course," Art said, seeing no reason why they wouldn't.

As John held Clara, he thought of the Greenes of Levit-town; if he could love her like *that*, whatever that inimitable way was, then she would be fine.

The twenty-year-old next to him on the plane burrowed protectively into her magazine. John cuddled Clara like the furrier would.

The cab from Kennedy let them out on Canal, across the street from where they'd originally departed. The baby was hot but asleep on his chest. Crosby Street was the same dark snowy block he'd left on Friday morning. He walked north toward their building, the gray sky flecked with bits of freezing rain. The same stack of take-out menus jammed the door as he pushed it open. His heart pounded in the small elevator, which smelled of someone's workout. Of course, it would not be normal to see her. For an instant he couldn't recall her face, the precise line of her jaw or the shape of her nose. He was terrified.

With great relief and disappointment, he found the apartment empty. Her lemony perfume hung in the air of the bathroom. A damp towel fell off a doorknob. He was relieved to find more pink medicine in the cabinet above the microwave and fresh goat milk in the fridge. He fed Clara, put her in the red Bugaboo stroller, and rolled her around the buffed concrete floors until she fell asleep. How long was it, fifteen minutes, twenty? Another deferment. His daughter was always doing this, stretching the distance between him and his own needs. He'd had no time to use the bathroom, let alone shower.

But then the intercom sounded, and John answered it quickly after half a buzz so it wouldn't wake Clara.

"Hello?" he said. Someone breathed. "Hello?" he said again over the fuzz.

"John?" Veronica sounded vaguely hoarse, as if hungover. He felt his chest opening, fluttering like it did when they'd first met, every time she spoke to him, and especially when she said his name.

"Yeah, it's me."

Sunday

Veronica

The intercom's static made it sound like an overseas connection. He buzzed her in. Somehow she'd been unable to go home unannounced. Through the glass, she saw Muriel nod and drive away.

Veronica entered the elevator and pressed the button. The magical box rose, yet a small eternity bloomed as she waited for the doors to reopen. When they finally did, she saw only John; his face was pinker than she remembered it, and his hair was wilder, as if it had grown over the weekend. He held a finger to his lips to quiet her. She looked quickly past him, scanning the room until the red stroller came into view, and in it the large, nearly bald head of her daughter. *"Thank God!"* she said. Standing above the stroller, she watched Clara's mouth moving on her pacifier, her plump cheeks working as she rested under a thin flannel blanket.

"She's *fine*," John said, approaching Veronica.

"What about you? You—you lied to me," she said, truly more confused than angry. She noticed the white sectional, which they never sat on, with its stiff arrangement of slate pillows. It was a sterile room, unwelcoming and cold. "You said you were at your mother's." She walked toward the kitchen island and placed her purse on the marble counter. She steadied herself there against the cool veined stone, unable to look up at him. "Where were you?" She came closer to him. For a moment she thought she would hug him, to see that he was real.

"Shhhh," he said.

"Did you just shush me?" She touched his chest and pushed. She saw the shock in his face as he stumbled backward into the blank whiteness of the loft.

"Sorry, but Clara's *asleep*," he hissed.

Sleep was the thing—miraculous in its erasure, magnanimous in its blessings.

"I went to Irvington and you weren't there." She spoke tentatively again, with the intonation of a question. Was he still capable of persuading her of something defensible?

"Can you listen?" he asked, and his defensiveness bothered her.

"Do you know how humiliating it was to see your old room? It was almost endearing until I discovered you had never slept in it!" It was then that she noticed a large, plum-shaped bruise emerging from his hairline. He looked rougher, ravaged. Maybe he'd been hurt or fallen. "Oh my God. What happened to you?"

"I'm fine, I—I'm sorry," he said. A small tremble started in his lower lip as he touched the bruise. He still was a boy. It was uncanny; he was not a boy *in disguise* as a man, as she'd charitably imagined, but an actual child.

But he was her boy. Something or someone had struck him. She waited for him to speak.

"I'm sorry. Listen to me. I tried to reach you. Where were *you?*"

"Nowhere," she said, heat rising to her cheeks. "That's not the point." She spoke more softly now, chastened. She felt his eyes on her, lingering on her mouth, then breasts. His mouth was ragged, an inverted slash with a dark shadow of stubble surrounding it. Above the bruise his hairline was caked with a thin maroon line of dried blood. She took his hands in her own. "Were you in an accident?"

"I was hit on the head with a ball. I almost got a concussion."

"*Almost?* What sort of ball?"

He looked at the floor. She dropped his hands.

"You went off to Amherst, with the baby? Why didn't you tell me?" She was still in her coat. Boiling, she flung it off.

"No," he said, perching on a kitchen stool. He closed his eyes and then looked at the ceiling for a long moment.

"What do you mean, *no?* We never do that, just go with the baby without talking to each other. Is she all right?" She saw his prominent Adam's apple bob up and down as he swallowed hard.

"I told you, she's fine. I called you last night."

Last night. It was a lucid dream that had become reality. She wished it were a dream. She walked past him to look down at Clara again, unable to face him. His familiar mouth was bleary at its edges, like a mouth in a Rembrandt. "When did she go down?" Veronica asked. She returned to lean against the cool marble island.

"A few minutes ago." He reached out and squeezed her shoulder. "I know you're mad, but I want you—I want you to understand," he said. Taking her by both shoulders, he grabbed her firmly and kissed her hard and fast.

"Don't!" she said, a vibration beginning to knock in her knees. Why did he always know her thoughts? His mouth came to hers as if he knew she'd thought about it. Despite everything—or perhaps because of it—desire had returned to her in his absence. They breathed hard, apart from each other, and she tasted salt from his kiss, felt the brief wetness from his tongue.

"I missed you," he said. "I went for you. Listen: I—I wanted you to get some sleep. Did you get some sleep?"

"Of course. Do you understand how tired I am? The chronic—"

He cut her off. "I know, I *do* know," he told her.

She picked up the note he'd left on the kitchen counter and shook her head. "How could you go without telling me? You took her—"

This time *he* averted his eyes. His gaze skittered away to the stroller, to the counter, to the door. She looked at his long eyelashes, the deeper pores around his nose, and for a moment they were simply mammals with hair, skin, and warm breath.

"I was going to take her out for breakfast," he said. He walked to the window and opened it, his breath steaming in the chilly air.

She crossed the room and shut it. "So as you were walking to the car and getting in, you didn't think—" She tried to proceed, but she couldn't really be righteous. She was massively relieved; they were all home together.

"I didn't drive. Listen, I don't want to wake her. Come and I'll tell you." He took her hand and pulled her with him. Alarmed by his strong grip, she wriggled free yet followed him out of the living room and into Clara's yellow nursery. He stood there breathing heavily as he leaned against the changing table.

She folded her arms over her chest as if she were simply annoyed, as she had been on Thursday night. But her anger was enervating. She sat on the crisp twin bed across from the empty crib, frail and depleted.

"I wasn't *in* Massachusetts," he said, almost angrily.

His face darkened. A shadow slid across his eyes. Had he been mugged? She was embarrassed for a moment. She'd misunderstood. He had been taken away, beaten up.

"What happened?"

He smiled at her then, a solicitous but sorrowful smile. The black fleck in his eye was as dense and sharp as India ink. "We went to Barbados."

It was a strangely simple phrase.

A loud snort emerged from her nose. "You did not!" Her own laughter, familiar in its rueful disbelief, calmed her for a moment.

He continued, almost eagerly, his eyes glittering. "I really did. *We* did."

The radiator clanked loudly. She saw the large dark freckle that always emerged on his collarbone when he was in the sun, the pinkish burn on the tops of his white hands where he always forgot to put lotion.

"What?"

He nodded.

"You did not! How did you do that?" Slopes of understanding were jagged in her brain. She fell from one to another. "What? What did you *do*? You went to the airport? You *took* her out—you— Holy fucking shit!"

"I didn't plan to," he said, sitting down on the glider. "It wasn't something I planned. I missed you so much. I *still* miss you."

"You actually went." It was hard to breathe, and her words were hushed, trancelike. "With Clara . . ." She stared at her black boots as they dug into the white sheepskin rug at her feet. It could not be. "I don't know where to begin."

"I can't really comprehend it either," he said, and she saw the odd glee in his face. He was excited by this shred of commonality, as if it were something to celebrate.

The room's edges were crisp and outlined, almost artificial. Their words, clattering objects. "Wait. You had plane tickets?"

"Well, no, not until I got to the airport, and then I got one ticket. There was one flight—" He had an infuriating smile on his face that she could tell he was trying to contain.

"You had passports. You're like one of those people who— you took her out of the country!" Veronica bent herself down over the pillow in her lap. She stared at his feet, both with sunburned tops. A few grains of sand rested on his big toe.

"I checked the mail as I was leaving and the passports were there. I didn't have tickets," he said, *"before."*

Veronica lifted her face. John and the window behind him blurred through her tears. "Oh my God." She covered her mouth with one hand and shook her head.

"I don't know. I just went."

"I'm her mother."

"I didn't plan it."

"It doesn't matter where I am; I know where she is—I know. I follow her whole day, her whole night, what she eats. When she wakes up from her nap. Everything! I do it! You don't do it. It's me."

"It's not only you—I go in there every night and check on her. I promise you, I took care of her."

Veronica's skull felt like it was simmering, lifting apart. "You go in there every night and wake her up when she's sleeping. You think that's checking on her?" She tore off her black sweater and threw it to the floor. The heat in the room, the heat within her, had become unbearable.

"I go in to make sure she's breathing! All right?"

"So that makes it better? You think you're like me? I go through the day and imagine her every minute, call Rosemary to ask about icing carrots for her gums and call back to tell her to make sure they're organic, and then hang up and think about how they can't be baby carrots, because she could choke on one and how they have to be full-sized carrots! Call again to ask what's in her diaper, hear about a reddish tinge, wonder if she had somehow ingested beets and worry that it's blood. You're proposing that you go through your day doing this too? Wondering about her stool when you should be working? I'm her mother. You go away and forget. You have your needs. *You* are paramount. To *you*. I don't have needs anymore. Do you even get that? I don't know if I am hungry or tired. I have no idea. I don't need a single goddamn thing!"

She tore out of the room and down the hallway. Reaching

the stroller where Clara slept, Veronica bent down and touched her forehead. It was burning up.

"That's total bullshit," John said, rushing after her. "You don't need a thing—you never think of yourself, is that what you're saying?"

She picked up the baby. "She's on fire."

"You never think of yourself? Then what the hell were you doing when she was two months old? What would you call that? Excellent parenting?"

"The Tylenol's above the microwave, up in that cabinet." Her tears started falling and she wiped them away. "You know I'm sorry. We've been through this," she said quietly. "Hurry up."

"But, see, we haven't been through it. Not really," he said, as he cracked open the seal on the tiny pink bottle.

"I fucked up. But I'm not a terrible mother." Finally, accidentally, she had asserted it. She did not have to wait for his verdict. "Please. Don't turn this into something else."

"It's not something else. Can't you see? *It's all one thing!*"

Veronica stood and swayed with Clara's hot, limp body in her arms. She stared into the stroller for the beloved lamb. With her free hand, she rummaged nervously under the stroller pads, then looked for it in the basket beneath the stroller, but the lamb was gone.

"You kidnapped her," she said, almost laughing with incredulity. She caught a drip from her nose with the back of her sleeve.

"I should have told you where I was." Veronica cradled Clara and, with her pinky, opened the baby's mouth. John administered the medicine.

"Okay," she said. She didn't know what to do with the impossible new information. He had acted without thinking, just as she had.

"Meanwhile, you've been fucking impossible," he said, renewing their argument.

"Art told me you think I'm crazy."

"I don't."

"You do. You think I'm a crazy bitch. And because of that— your own unfair characterization—that justifies . . . You said she was okay. How long has she had a fever?"

"She had a low one last night and some diarrhea."

"Were you even going to tell me that?"

"I was going to—I haven't had a chance. I know it was strange, leaving, I know, but it was also kind of *extraordinary*."

"Extraordinary?" She noticed that his eyes danced and shimmered, until she started to move toward him. With her free hand, she grabbed a pillow off the sofa and swung it at him. She felt his unshaved face against her palm, his nose and his oily hair. He shielded himself with his arms. A great lash of fire whipped up and through her, propelling her toward him. She yanked at the neck of his T-shirt and held on.

"Extraordinary! Wow. It was extraordinary to lie to your wife and take your baby to a foreign country without telling her?" He looked at her hand on his shirt. "And now she's sick?" She hadn't had this much energy since she was pushing, trying to get Clara out into the world; like a tidal wave her whole body was washed and lit.

Yet before she could say any more, a feeling of sheer defeat gripped her; in that effort, despite that singular energy, she'd failed. She let go of his shirt, walked across the room to get the thermometer and take the baby's temperature. The thermometer beeped and read 101. It wasn't as high as she'd guessed.

"You were sick and overtired and I thought you'd needed to rest for a *long* time. You needed a break. That's all I wanted," he said, as if their world were still cohesive. "I never wanted you to be hurt. I tried to protect you; even in the hospital I tried to do everything for you. I would do anything. Anything you want. I didn't plan on going there."

She moved down the hall with Clara in her arms.

He followed her to the door of the nursery and watched as she put the baby in the crib. Clara's lack of protest was worrisome. "Listen. It's me, Veronica." He was standing, his nostrils flaring, his arms open, as if ready to capture her. "It's me."

"Whatever that means. What does that mean?" She stood there, burning, fluttering as if a million birds beat their wings in her chest. She could have run in giant steps, scaling Manhattan, the earth. She could have flown. "Who are you?"

They were silent for what seemed like a long time. An old Snoopy digital clock John had salvaged once from Irvington made its loud click from one minute to the next. An impossible distance. Dust motes shivered around the air purifier near the window. An ambulance screamed. Two people walked by on the street and their conversation floated up: "Did he get the bacon?" one woman asked. The other assured her friend: "He did." How Veronica wished they were talking about bacon.

"I admit it must seem strange to you," he finally said in a choked voice, a meager concession. But she wasn't ready to comfort him.

It was disconcerting how John wouldn't look away, how he stared at her. Something hummed there between them like a moving painting, something that breathed when you didn't expect it to. From the airing came a strange mutual relief.

"I'm not crazy," he said.

"You left me," she said, as if aware of it from a different angle.

"That's what Derek said."

"Who's he?"

"A friend."

When had he had a friend she didn't know? "I suppose you went to Glittering Sands."

"I tried to, but they wouldn't let me in."

Veronica shook her head.

"Veronica," he said, "listen."

"No, I will not listen to you!" She could not. She had to get away from him. But when she moved to go through the door, he blocked her path.

17

Sunday
John

He could not let her go. He had to tell her what had happened, how he'd finally understood, how valiantly he'd searched for goat milk. The dream of the white flower in her hair, the dialogue with his father: It was all fueled by love for her. "Where are you going?"

"Away."

She tried to squeeze past him, under his arm, but he held her there, prying her hand off the knob. He didn't let go. Her wrist felt stiff in his grasp, like polished wood. She smelled clean, her hair freshly washed with some new shampoo.

"Let me go, okay?" He heard a crack of fear in her voice.

He held on to her. "I will not let you go," he said. He needed to tell her everything. He felt her body grow tense beneath his hands. He looked at her white neck and wanted to nibble it; that used to happen so easily and was now so improbable. Lately she would never let him touch her. Now he could imagine it again; he could devour her.

"Let me go, John, okay? Let go." She spoke pleadingly, gently. He held on tighter, his fingers sinking into the flesh of her wrists. A softening had emerged in her voice; her words were peeled and alert. In this state, maybe he could reach her; maybe she could finally hear him.

"No. *I need you*," he said. He was too tired to think straight. For months she had been this way, withholding and unreachable. She was simply evasive because he was touching her, like she always was. His mind darted close to and then away from knowledge: She was leaving him. She would be gone, as he had feared the night of the birth, as he feared in the subsequent months of her coolness and removal. His mind was going to the darkest places. He took shelter in something simple: lust and the pleasant awareness of his size compared with hers. His relative power.

"Please get off," she said, almost formally this time, yet he thought he detected a break in her resolve. He pushed her securely against the frame of the door, pinning her with his hips. Her Botticelli face was raw, pale, and very awake.

"Please, V," he said. He kissed her chest near her collarbone, then her breast through the fabric of her tank top.

"Don't," she said. He kissed her other breast, her clavicle. She had to let him. She stepped on his foot, which he felt was mildly encouraging—footsie—until she stepped again, hard, with the heel of her boot. The door frame held them there as his foot throbbed.

"I'm not going anywhere," he said.

"You already did."

He pressed the top of his head into her neck, nuzzling and inhaling her.

1 8

Sunday

Veronica

What happened next was unexpected. A familiar scent rose up around her, warm and sweet. It was coconut oil, rich and intoxicating. She saw a smear of it on the neck of his T-shirt. She sniffed it. The triangular patch of light behind his head melted and broke open. She leaned closer to him as if into a darkening prism. Winter sunlight poured into the space of the doorway, warming the crown of her head, her hair. She stopped pushing him away. She breathed him in.

Her body loosened in his arms. "Are you okay?" he asked. She couldn't speak. Last night had been a mistake, an aberration. She nodded and pulled him closer to her. She was overcome quite suddenly by that fleeting, strange lover's conceit that they were one and, having been unnaturally parted, they would—*had to*—connect. This was what was real.

He pulled her back into the nursery with a proprietary

hand on the nape of her neck and shut the door. "The baby!" she said, almost demurely, knowing that she wasn't going to go to her, that instead she would have sex with her insane husband. His aggressive motions became tender. Down the hall, Clara cried out briefly. John opened Veronica's jeans fast with one hand and traced a finger on the rim of her underwear, just above the scar. They were the lemon-yellow lacy ones, nicer than any underwear she'd worn for months, which she had put on Saturday morning a million eons ago. She felt him touch the edge of the panties, almost mournfully, before he yanked them down.

She kissed him more deeply and he pressed his hands under her shirt, under her filmy bra onto her nipples, which hardened quickly beneath his fingertips. There was no time—the baby might wake up—but it was as if they were saying hello and goodbye at once, and it had to be *at once*, very fast and immediate.

The sheepskin rug was soft beneath her. His white narrow hips were a delectable blade, a part of a machine, burrowing in, while his stubbly chin knocked at her jawbone and neck. Sorrow consumed her.

"What is it?" He paused above her, sensing her distraction.

"Nothing." She swam in this warmth. His hair, the oil, his skin. Saturated yellow glowed beneath her eyelids. Yellow turned brighter and deeper into gold. The color seared through her like something electric, a flash of happiness.

The spell ended as quickly as it had begun. The golden hue was eclipsed by darkness. In the back of her throat she could still taste Damon's licorice toothpaste. What had she done? She heard John say, "I'm sorry. What's wrong?" Her cheek rested in his warm palm. She hesitated there. Despite all that had happened, the grave flight away from each other, the otherworldly delusions, he was holding her the way she had always wanted to be held.

He caressed the brown curve of her hips. She saw him move back a bit, perhaps to gain perspective. She recognized the question in his face: Was this the last time, or had she forgiven him? He cupped her face in his hands. "You look so sad," he said.

"You have no idea—" she answered, as tears spilled from her closed lids.

Clara woke up and cried in earnest. Neither one of them moved to get her.

1 9

Sunday

John

It wasn't the baby but the telephone that roused them. "Don't go away," John told Veronica before rushing to answer the call, to stop the ringing and get rid of it—whoever it was—because he needed to return quickly to that sheepskin rug, while she was still there, while her great distress made her available. He picked up the kitchen phone.

"Ines may be miscarrying again. She's bleeding," Art said, trumping them and their own domestic drama. Veronica, half dressed, rushed out of the nursery and over to the stroller, pushing it a few times until Clara settled down. *You have no idea,* she'd said. Now he'd lost his chance for discovery. "We're at the hospital," Art said, "and if you could come by—actually, if *Veronica* could come."

"Let me get her," John said, and he motioned for Veronica to pick up the other phone. He recalled Art's single-word response: WHAT? He was glad that he'd been temporarily forgotten.

Veronica picked up in the bedroom. When she heard, she asked about the blood. "Was it bright red or brown?"

"The second one, I guess," Art said sheepishly. "She said it was like at the end of your period. I don't know exactly."

"Good, that's a *good* thing," she said, though her voice wavered.

The fear from the hospital—that long spell of uncertainty—returned to John. From the kitchen he watched Veronica through the open bedroom door as she quickly got dressed. She paused, hands on her hips, the phone in the crook of her neck, before she peeled off the yellow lacy underpants, replacing them with some white cotton ones.

Art said, "They said it was too early for Braxton Hicks, whatever that is." John didn't know what it meant either. He didn't know what any of it meant—how you could thoughtlessly have sex for decades with no repercussions, how the mysteries of biology could mean nothing to you and then, quite suddenly, dominate your life.

"I'll leave right now. Have you been seen yet?" Veronica asked.

"Not yet. We'll be here awhile. Ines said she wanted every test under the sun." Art's voice was stripped, sad, the way John had rarely heard it.

John hung up and found Veronica already fastening Clara onto her body. "Her fever's down. Hopefully we'll be back soon," she said, rushing to the door.

"Leave Clara here with me." Ordinarily that's what they'd do. It was close to her bath time and she'd been sick.

"I just can't," she said, her face shrouded by her marvelous hair.

"I'm coming with you, then." He could not let her go. He followed her out the door. She adjusted the baby's socks—made to look like Mary Jane shoes—as they rode down in the elevator. He'd been briefly optimistic, but Veronica was as distant, as she'd seemed on her first day back to work months ago, capable and clearheaded when faced with problems that weren't her own.

On the street, she let him hold her hand briefly as they walked to the corner, but then she removed it to fidget with the carrier. "It seems more serious than it is. They're only going to the hospital because it's a Sunday. On a weekday they'd just be sent to her doctor's office," she told him, thinking aloud.

They jumped into a cab on Spring Street. As they rode uptown, they must have looked ordinary to anyone—a family of three heading out together on a Sunday afternoon. They had been that family, and all the while—through the unseasonably hot fall, through the darkness of winter, through the virtual weekend and the dream of escape—he had not fully known this.

"Did Art know where you went?" she asked.

"Art? He had no idea," he said, unsure why he lied.

"He must have," she said, shaking her head.

"He had nothing to do with it. If you'd let me, I'd tell you everything."

"Your mother definitely had no idea. She told me that story

about you visiting the Sandlemans when you were little—she loves that story."

"She does," he said, but Veronica had turned away from him to look out the window at the slush in Union Square. "I'm here," he said, breathing into her shoulder, "in case you want to keep talking." Briefly, she turned to him. "I missed you," he said.

"I missed you too."

The cab passed the dowdy restaurants on First Avenue where he'd eaten far too many meals, the mediocre pizza places and the bars patronized by hospital staff in dirty white lab coats; passed the entrance to the Midtown Tunnel and the endless rows of doctors' offices with brass plaques until they were back at the hospital, back where Clara had been born.

He liked feeling Veronica follow him out of the car and around the corner as they walked under the neon EMERGENCY sign and into the fluorescent waiting room.

His newly able wife approached the desk.

"Arthur Greene is already with the patient; you can't go back," a nurse told her.

"She asked for me," Veronica said, "specifically."

John remembered the greyhound running through the lavender, the poster that read EXCELLENCE. He had once taken care of her.

"Only one significant other."

"Can you let her know I'm here?" They waited. Veronica paced with Clara, who was twisting in her sling, on the verge of a meltdown.

Just as she did on the night of Clara's birth, Veronica had to keep moving. If she paused for a moment or dared to sit down, the baby would be incensed.

Across the East River, the Pepsi-Cola sign was still beating like a heart. The hysterectomy had brought him this same view and the odd refreshment of the air outside the building. Now they were together, looking at the same sign from the same vantage point; they were together in a place where he could have lost them both.

"Listen. I can get the medical records from Berlin's office." It came to him suddenly, the way she might return, the way she might forgive him. She'd been calling Berlin's office for months, asking for the birth record; she had sent and signed all the required forms, but they would not release it.

"That's nice of you." She smiled faintly, which was encouraging. "But it doesn't matter anymore," she added.

"It doesn't matter anymore?" What had happened during the birth had mattered to her for months. He had just caught up to that fact; he'd finally understood.

"They wouldn't give them to you, anyway." She spoke without bitterness. "You're not the patient."

"I'm going to go there in person and demand the damn thing."

She looked at him as he kept pace beside her. "It has to be me."

"I'll go with you, then. We'll go together one day at lunch."

She stopped walking. "At lunch?" she said with a note of confusion. They never had lunch together. Above her, a TV hung from the ceiling in the corner; there, a weatherman was pointing at a dark-gray cloud flecked with flurries.

"Well, we should," he said. She was right. All they did was work.

He approached Veronica as she turned to stare at the television. He spoke into her hair. "I love you," he said. Clara started to fuss. She whipped around, standing back to assess him. Her pale eyes roamed over his face as she bit her lower lip. "Can I hold the baby now?" he asked.

"No way," she said. "Can you get me a coffee, though?"

At the moment, nothing could have made him happier than this mundane request.

20

Sunday

Veronica

The rage that had begun, sweeping her up in its grasp, had been tiring; it was like wrestling with a tangled kite in the wind. White noise and motion and no release. If you held on, the rope would burn your hand. But if you let go of it, the kite would just fly away. She couldn't let go of it yet.

When he left for the coffee, there was reprieve in the form of the weatherman on TV pulling down a cumulous cloud, delivering the predictable report on barometric pressure and snow. Ines's fate was unpredictable: There she was beyond those double doors in one of those insufficient hospital gowns that kept opening in the back, imagining a future she did not yet, might not ever, possess. Veronica was now holding her child, cool and calm on her chest.

Theirs was a different sort of emergency from Ines's. For

months John had moped around the loft on weekends in the same thin red flannel shirt, playing Scrabble on the computer. He also played solitaire, and a few times she'd caught him inside virtual realities, fighting demons and vanquishing enemies with unusual cyber monikers. All those nights she had spared telling him that she'd noticed what he "worked on," and she—well, she'd gone to bed early to read the side effects and warning labels on her various prescriptions. She'd keep the light on for him, trying to wait up but never could. *He* had betrayed her too. They had not gone anywhere for months.

Then on Friday he'd left her, his work, his rut. He had taken the baby away from her. It was unconscionable. He had gone away; he had in fact *done* something. And John had returned with a new energy. She couldn't deny that she felt it. How would he conceive of it? He was a bold explorer, a brave knight who had conquered an unknown land. She had needed him to stay, to be with her regardless of her mood.

The weatherman's snow disappeared from the TV screen; in its place, a fleet of Humvees drove across a desert. Clara finally succumbed to sleep and Veronica sat down to rest. A nurse in aqua scrubs scribbled on a clipboard while a gold locket dangled in her cleavage. Inside the locket, no doubt, there was a picture of *her* beloved. All experience was subjective. Veronica—as she had been in Ines's kitchen on Friday night— was a speck in a vast universe. She was nothing more than a mass of cells floating in darkness. She hovered there, unmoored, wondering how long the feeling could last.

When she saw John returning with the coffee, everything mattered again; his face warmed at the sight of her. She could not have gotten through the birth without his unseasoned and terrified care. "Thank you," she said.

"You're welcome."

"I'm worried about that bruise on your forehead." She touched it gently. Iodine and blood caked his hairline. She had let go.

"Are you?"

"I'm worried about Ines too," she said.

"I think she'll be all right. I do, I do," he said, protesting too much. He opened his coffee. Steam surrounded his face as he watched the TV. She, too, had gone away. She had been cut, turned into a set of parts. But the sum, *the sum of the parts,* remained.

"How many nights were we here? Was it two or did it turn into three?"

John blew his drink. The coffee was too hot to touch. "Nine, if you count your week of recovery."

"Was it that bad?"

"It could've been."

They rested there and cautiously sipped. It was their first effortless moment together in months. She knew it could be their last.

Before they finished their coffee, Arthur bounded out. "She needs bed rest for a few days and then—well, then she should be fine," he said. He and John hugged each other before he hugged Veronica too tightly, lightly crushing the baby between them.

"What did they say?" Veronica asked.

"It was what they thought. Some fluid. Leaking. The

placenta is leaking, so it needs to repair. To heal. If she rests, it's supposed to heal."

Ines then emerged, looking pale and almost chastened.

"Hey," she said, leaning into Veronica. "Thanks for coming. The baby, according to the sonogram, is fine. Who knew! I need to rest for five days and then be seen again."

"I'm so relieved," Veronica said. She hugged Ines, haunted by the extreme delicacy of a life. "Should we go put you to bed? Can we bring you some dinner?"

"No, no, we're good," Ines said.

"We're so *not* good," Art said. "Come over and we'll order Thai. It will be good for your hangover," he said, looking at Veronica.

John glanced at her. "We got a little drunk," she said. Her cyber moniker: Lusty Liver.

During dinner, Veronica was a helper. She helped, bringing Ines a pitcher of water for her bedside and a tray of dinner, emptying Ines's trash, and straightening up for the days of convalescence ahead. Clara, up ridiculously late, lay on floor playing with Art's red Puma. The two men were in the living room. For the first time since they'd met, Veronica didn't confide in Ines. The bedroom, the black modernist chair in the corner—Dr. Weiss had had the same one—the framed poster of a movie by Antonioni, Ines sitting in her bed and eating pad Thai, was the last hiding place.

They lingered there, inside the larger, more-forgiving unit: friendship. Clara drank a bottle and fell asleep in her mother's arms as Veronica sat in that black chair. They left when Art announced that he was going to bed.

In the elevator, John's earlier solicitousness had vanished. He leaned in one corner, holding the railing as if for balance and staring stonily at the floor. He was *physically* so familiar to her. Yes, she knew this body, but what was he thinking? How had his mood changed so quickly? His body was this mysterious container, this shield, yet it was all she could see. She reached up and touched his cheek, and he pushed her hand away. Mystery was romantic, but this total mystery, his withdrawal, was shattering. Finally he looked up. "Art mentioned you ran into Satan," he said.

"No we didn't," she said. Later she would regret this simple lie.

She looked up at each lit number as they descended. If they could just get to the lobby and out of this space.

"How drunk were you?"

"What? Well, a bit drunk, I suppose." The enclosed space grew smaller, its wood paneling marbled with age, with years and years of arguments and wax, shattering news, polite silences, followed by good shiny rubbings.

"So did you see him or not?"

"Yes, I guess we did. He was at Isabella's," she said, trying not to visibly crumble.

"He was?" he said.

She was aware that her innocence was over. "My shoulders are killing me," she muttered, adjusting the straps of the carrier and looking away again, this time up to the honeycomb grate on the light fixture. There were little golden octagons, as if bees would buzz out and she and John could open their mouths and catch honey on their tongues.

They passed 3 and then 2. "Then why'd you say he wasn't?" John asked, pressing 17.

"Because I forgot."

"You forgot?"

"Nothing happened," she said. She needed him to stop this. She was never going to tell him.

"Who said anything happened? Wait—"

She started to shake lightly, holding on to the sleeping baby to steady herself.

"Well, Art said you did see him and that he's still a complete prick," he added, his eyes on her.

Had his uncertainty faded, pivoting into knowledge? But she hadn't let on, she hadn't said a word.

"I suppose he is," she answered quietly. "I don't know." She looked at the numbers, which had reached 5 again when John pressed 16.

"Can you stop doing that? I just want to go home."

"You didn't answer the phone last night when I called."

"I told you, I ate dinner with Art and Ines."

"They were home asleep by ten. What the hell? *You* tell me, Veronica. Is he a complete prick?" The elevator hit the lobby and she started to head for the door. He shoved her back and smashed his hand over the numbers, pressing a couple at once. The lit box zoomed back up expertly, quietly, to 5; with a gentle ping, the doors opened briefly to a mirrored foyer and then closed and catapulted to 8.

John kept pressing buttons, staring, demanding her answer. "You tell me."

She ignored him as tears fell freely now in a soundless, unstoppable torrent, and reached across him and pressed the *L* button for the lobby, with what were perhaps the last traces of the cold composure of *after.*

"There's nothing to tell. Please," she said, imploring him to free her, to let it go.

"I know you," he said. "Don't you see that?" She had never meant to do it. "You tell me!" She faced him, his amber eyes pinned to hers. He let the elevator sink to its descent while she told him. Like the last bit of sand in an hourglass, it came out surprisingly straight and fast, the unadorned fact of her betrayal.

As the words escaped, she saw his face change completely; like a paper bag, it collapsed around the hollow of his mouth. The roses drained from his cheeks. His eyes were glassy inside their newly bony sockets, the very presentiment of death. She wanted to go to him, to help him, but he was gone.

Six Days Later

John

It was not Evan who watched approvingly while John said no to butter on his popcorn; Veronica had become the ghost. She approved of the dry popcorn but not the movie—the sequel to a cult thriller. She was the only person he knew who could fall asleep during a car chase. How he had loved that, her fragrant hair resting on his shoulder, her sleep complete and deep. And her explanation for it later was something he knew was cogent, even extremely intelligent, but he couldn't remember, because he had been too busy staring at her lips as she explained how boring and predictable a car chase actually was. He accepted the bottled water he'd purchased instead of a Coke, pocketed the change, and then stood there, unsure of what he was waiting for. Art came and stood in his line of vision.

"Oh, man," Art said, "we have got to get you a good shrink."

"I'm fine. I guess I could use a drink." It was Saturday night and Veronica had been uptown for four nights. He had asked for some time alone. But the weekend was enormous, monstrously long. She had to come back.

"No, a *shrink*! Not a *drink*," Art said. "You're crying again. I don't know if you realize that."

It had been happening a lot; he'd be buying a newspaper or walking in to the subway or taking a shower, and he wouldn't convulse, but his eyes would fill, then overflow without a sound. After his initial rage, he didn't have much to say to go with these tears. He was heartbroken, dumbfounded.

"I can't believe I'm a *cuckold*. Here." He offered Art the popcorn. "I got this for us—no butter, for my gut."

"Good boy. She's *not* here. See, one of the advantages of this time apart would be actually *getting* the butter. *Getting* the steak."

"I don't want the steak, okay?"

"Jeez!"

Art was able to lay off it once they'd found their seats. The stereo boomed its deafening ads. Ads on movie screens? He remembered the feel of Veronica's head on his shoulder. When they'd met, there were no ads before movies. There was a past, and it contained such beauty.

John fidgeted in his seat, threatening to explode. The explosion ended as it always did within his uncomprehending mind: How could she do it? He had been away for only two nights. There was a gaping hole in his life, an error that didn't compute.

All week he'd been scrambling to catch up at work; he'd fallen behind on two due dates. He told Lloyd Miller that he'd had to go visit his mother. But it didn't matter. What mattered was that his report on Lancelot's sleep aid was sloppy. Miller said it lacked clarity and the data on Lancelot's earnings was disorganized.

In the name of research, John now took a pill every night, curling to sleep on the awful sofa to avoid sleeping alone in their bed. Veronica's affection, her sweet depth, that Sunday afternoon reunion, had been so unexpected. He tried to remember the tenderness of their encounter. Was it real? It was. Then, retrospectively, knowing what he now knew, it wasn't. Finally, the yellow underwear destroyed him. He tortured himself thinking about it and wondering if Damon had noticed it too.

Derek had called and left a message on the machine, and John had been avoiding calling him back. He fucking hated Derek. Derek had said it: "You left her?" And he was right. If he hadn't left, none of this would have happened. Yes, he had told her to go, but the wait, the open-ended separation, was becoming unbearable.

As Art and John walked east on Houston after the movie, people everywhere held phones to their ears or thumbed them in their palms, as if those devices could actually connect you to a person. Art asked John what he thought of the movie, but it had begun and ended without him being able to follow the plot. They walked in silence before Art said, "You don't have to sit in a bar with me with tears running down your face, okay? Go home. I'll walk you there."

"What are *you* going to do?" John asked, bereft to the point of confusion, his own voice like cotton in his dry mouth.

"I'll have one beer, then go home. Man, listen, you need a plan, something very definitive, to tell her what it is you want, that you want her back. Practice saying it. She'll listen to you. Women like that, being pursued."

"How could she do this to me?" he said, but as he said it, he saw Art's eyes roll just a bit. Soft breezes had tickled his face and neck when he saw Monika standing there with her strong tanned legs. Despite his exhaustion, despite everything, he *had* desired her. Desire was like a sweet tooth, a pull. It was human.

"You have to put Satan out of your mind. You've got to tell her you want her. Woo her."

"There has to be, like, this waiting period. I'm punishing her, I guess." There were glimmers of hope. Her remorse was full and he could tell, almost confusing to her, as if she were truly a person who had been overcome, who had stepped briefly into another life and was surprised by what she'd done. She had asked forgiveness and had put Clara up to the phone to hear her dad's voice. She called often and said she was worried about him. The lights of the street doubled, jumping ahead of him through wet eyes. He passed a homeless man on Thompson Street and gave him five dollars. Veronica always admired this kind of generosity.

He would have to explain it to her, the way she was there even when she was not. Her vision had become a part of his own. Memory, the cascade of years, made time elastic, and everything they'd shared—watching a car chase in 1994, or refilling a wipe warmer in 2004—was converging. They had been young and slept late and now they were somnambulant, so tired they were practically dreaming as they moved. That was all Barbados had been: a lucid dream. He'd tell her eventually. She had to understand this: There was no absolute starting point. He was old enough to see that all of experience was one shimmering mass, fluid, not static. *Before* and *after* was a fiction.

The Same Night

Veronica

The sun set at four-forty on Saturday. Veronica watched it disappear, sinking into the reservoir, set up Clara with a life-size Italian leather pig on the floor of the Edelsons' kitchen, and started to cook some sweet potato for the baby's dinner. John's face, the shocked hollow of his mouth, stayed with her. She poured the last bit of white wine into a glass, took a sip, and then reconsidered, dumping it down the drain.

She'd arrived uptown on a Tuesday and Annalena had been out. Veronica had harbored a sliver of hope that her mother would be there for her with comforting words and all the right distractions for Clara though this was completely unlikely. *"Accept reality as it is, not as you want it to be,"* Dr. Weiss had repeated; Veronica was alone. John was too. They were not one. But they had once chosen to be together.

The pot bubbled on the stove. The waiting was terrible.

She understood how John felt but couldn't help him. He would relent, but what if by some accident of fate, or stubbornness, he didn't?

After dinner, she put Clara to bed in the guest room with the bumblebee wallpaper. She held the baby and went through their lengthy bedtime routine with the bottle, the short narration of the days' events, the incessant pacing while reciting hypnotizing words about sleep. Finally, at the point when Clara began to droop, cleaving to her mother's neck and shoulders, Veronica felt like she was splintering from the inside with hunger. It was true, what she'd told John: She often didn't know what she needed, didn't know whether she was hungry or tired, but now she was feeling those things again, bumping into them as they prickled up like crocuses beneath a deep freeze. She was starving. *Go to sleep*, she willed her daughter, *go to sleep.*

That first night, when Annalena and David finally came in, her father grabbed her by the shoulders to "take a look at her," he said. The firmness of his warm hands made her want to cry. Annalena glanced at Veronica and pronounced her "just fine." For the first time, her mother's flat assessment didn't crush her.

David's gray eyes scanned her face; then he kissed both cheeks. "Did you want to stay in your apartment? If you wanted to stay there and he wouldn't leave, I can take care of it."

"No, Daddy. It's not like that," she said, chilled by his intimation. She knew John could not understand her. Could he forgive her?

"Your name's on the title, right? I'm going to give you

Steve Shappel's number right now before I forget." He put the lawyer's card, a thick creamy thing, in Veronica's hand as if it were simply a referral for a dry cleaner or a salon, for any ordinary service.

The days continued in their gray hourly unfurling. After work one afternoon there was the plush solace of the Frick, where Veronica stared at an Ingres painting of a woman in a gray silky dress staring straight back at her. When the weekend had come, Annalena and David went to Delaware and left Veronica and Clara in the apartment.

She unwrapped some tofu to add to the sweet potato, cutting it into tiny cubes. There was no parallel world, no island or surreal painting in which to enact another life. It was a life of consequence and connection. She cut her finger and wrapped it in a paper towel to stanch the wound. Clara looked puzzled, watching her mother weep without restraint. She had to act.

At four o' clock on Sunday, before her parents returned, Veronica left. Fresh snow had fallen everywhere while she'd been inside. Powdery and silent, it already blanketed cars, stoops, and mailboxes. A little boy in a red coat held his tongue out in the air to catch it, his footsteps muffled beside her. The snow seemed pure, as if immune to the fact that this was a city. It was ignorant and lovely in its even democratic covering, painted like sugar glaze on dark-chocolate branches, crystallizing around the edges of fenders and benches. It must have been snowing downtown too, immaculate on the cobblestones of Crosby Street, fine and evenly sifted as flour on the rooftops of Lafayette, and on his shoulders too, the sadness of his exposed sunburned neck as he fumbled for his keys outside their door.

Fifth Avenue was nearly deserted. A lone white gypsy cab rattled softly by, and far away a woman walked a large black poodle. Eventually a bus came. She hesitated as the doors hissed open—she didn't know how she would find him—and a puff of heat tumbled out, surrounding her, an invitation.

Three Months Later

John and Veronica

Cheerios were all over the floor. The baby sat in the high chair, picking them up one by one in her thumb and fore-finger with grave concentration, like a jeweler holding a gem in a tweezer. The baby's mother lay on the rug on the floor a distance away, her arm flung over her eyes. She'd been up since five-twenty, reading the interminable *Busytown*. The baby's father was in the shower. It was eight-ten and he had made his offer: John had slept in, so now he would get up and take Clara to breakfast and the new playground in Battery Park while Veronica rested or did whatever she wanted to do. It sounded fair enough. But she was wired from two coffees. What did she want to do? Her will was sometimes indiscern-ible, still connected, as ever, to the baby's ever-expanding needs. Veronica was overambitious and dreamy; she wanted industry—perhaps she would finally clean out their hall closet or even go in to the office—and she wanted to crawl back into bed with the newspaper.

She'd take a bath, then decide. She lifted Clara from the high chair and went into the steamy bathroom, that marble vault, to turn it on. John stood shaving, moving with enviable leisure. "Good," he said, noticing the running water, "you should do that." She followed him out when he took Clara and snapped her into her stroller.

It was April and Soho was shimmering, the leaves newly green, footsteps echoing up to the third floor loft while John thought about a sweater or a light jacket. There were tulips—red ones that she liked—at the corner deli, and he'd bring some back for her. He put on the navy-blue sweater and tucked a pink blanket over the baby. Veronica crouched down to adjust it, then went to get him a sippy cup of water, a diaper and wipes, and finally a cotton hat. She stood twisting her fingers, watching him collect his keys and wallet. "When will you be back?" she asked.

"Soon," he said. They kissed, and he felt her tighten her hug for an extra moment before he left.

She lingered at the window and watched for their arrival on the street. She followed the red stroller with her eyes as they moved north to the diner. She swept up the cereal and then— she couldn't help it—put on a jacket and went outside. She ran to catch up with them. The spring air was refreshing on her face and neck; the assault of winter was over. "I thought I'd walk you there," she said, out of breath, when she caught up to him.

"We're here now," he said a moment later. There they stood. The sunshine moved behind a cloud, then darted out again as she adjusted the shade on the baby's stroller. Light dappled the space between them, shifting quickly from a glare to an ominous cool and back again. "Are you coming in?" he asked. Lately he didn't want to be away from her.

The day opened before her, full of possibility. She smelled the damp, floury smell of fresh bread. She shook her head. "No, you go ahead." There was an ancient mosaic on the floor of the Metropolitan Museum of Art. It was surrounded by thin brown ropes to protect it from viewers who might step too close. The security measure made it look like the most stunning crib. She would go back first to change her clothes. She watched her husband and daughter briefly as they went through the glass door to the diner; then she turned and found her way home.

Acknowledgments

I'm grateful to my parents, Lorna and Ed Goodman, who always surrounded me with books, for their love, patience and good faith; my sister, Sara, for being my longtime champion; Mott Hupfel for his tenacity; the Daltons, Olivers, and Elaine Sivcoski for enthusiasm and respect; and Mary Ann and Bruno Quinson and Pam Lichty for reading my work. All my friends have sustained me in myriad ways, but Jane Wagman, Jen Unter, Susanna Felleman, Hope Litoff, Niamh King, and Dianna Frid read the manuscript. Thank you to Tom Levinson and Elizabeth Kieff for seeing me through the long haul and then being there with champagne.

I thank Don Reneau, who read beginning chapters with interest and a sharp eye; Dalia Rabinovich, who was there early on; and Nell Freudenberger for her excellent example and her generosity. Wendy Gimbel's constant guidance, talent, and humor have buoyed me countless times. Emily Gray Tedrowe, Gina Frangello, and Patrick Somerville have been essential to this book. I thank Eric Best, John Britton, Todd Pietri, and Oliver Ryan for informative talks. In the eleventh hour, Diana Chapman and Mary Dougherty provided needed encouragement and introduced me to the archetypal power of this story.

Elyse Cheney is a wonderful agent, unflagging and true, whose confidence inspires me. She and everyone in her office worked hard on my behalf. I thank those at Henry Holt, in particular Steve Rubin, Maggie Richards, and Barbara Jones, an incomparable editor; her talent, wry humor, and complete dedication touched every page of this book.

My young children proved their patience and gave unconditional love. Above all, I'm indebted to my husband, Eric Oliver, for reading with such loving bias, for his brilliant imagination, and for constant immeasurable support.

About the Author

THEA GOODMAN has received the Columbia Fiction Award, a Pushcart Prize Special Mention, and fellowships at Yaddo and Ragdale; her short stories have appeared in several journals, notably *New England Review*, *Other Voices*, and *Columbia*. Born in New York City, she studied at Sarah Lawrence and earned her MFA from Brooklyn College, CUNY. She has taught writing at the School of the Art Institute of Chicago and lives in Chicago with her husband and children.